YULETIDE BLUES

YULETIDE BLUES

R.P. MacIntyre

Thistledown Press Ltd.

© Rod MacIntyre, 1991
Mass market edition, 1992
All rights reserved.

Canadian Cataloguing in Publication Data

MacIntyre, Rod, 1947-

Yuletide blues

ISBN 1-895449-04-9

I. Title.

PS8575.I67Y8 1992   jC813'.54   C92-098170-4
PZ7.M45Yu 1992

Book design by A.M. Forrie
Cover photo by Sean Francis Martin
Author photo by N. Collins
Typeset by Thistledown Press Ltd.

Printed and bound in Canada by
Webcom Ltd.
3480 Pharmacy Ave.
Scarborough,ON   M1W 3G3

Thistledown Press Ltd.
668 East Place
Saskatoon, Saskatchewan
S7J 2Z5

Acknowledgements

This book has been published with the assistance of
The Canada Council and the Saskatchewan Arts Board

*To Sharyn and Zoey
for their love and patience,
not necessarily in that order.*

CHAPTER ONE

My parents bought a piano five years ago. They gave it to me. "Here's your piano," they said. I never thought of it as mine personally. I don't think they did either. But that's the way it's always been, "Go practice your piano," they say, and "We didn't buy your piano to sit there and collect dust," etc., etc.

It's amazing that I can play it at all. I mean, look at it. What is it? It's this big wooden box with wires stretched inside. How it works is you bang on these white and black rectangular things that are attached to rows of little felt covered hammers that hit those stretched wires. And lo and behold, you get noise. If you do it right, you get music.

The only reason I think of this is because of this old guy who used to play the violin next door. Us kids used to call him Mr. Raisin because he used to eat them all the time and feed them to us. He said raisins were good for you, and I guess he would know because he looked like one too. You got to realize I was about five at the time and he was about a hundred. Anyway, he says, you stretch some cat guts across a hollow box, and you got a violin.

8 YULETIDE BLUES

Then you get some horsehair attached to a stick and call it a bow, and scrape the bow across the cat guts. What happens is you get music. "A miracle," he says. And I guess it really is amazing if you think about it, because in the old days they actually did use cat guts for violin strings.

I remember this because Mr. Raisin had about a dozen cats, and in my little five-year-old mind I had this incredible picture of this old guy doing very nasty things to his cats to make his music. It used to puzzle me too that cats had such thin guts after you put them on the violin because I knew a fresh dead cat, one that had just got hit by a truck, had guts that looked like thick red spaghetti. I used to feel sorry for all these dead cats that got used for making music. I still do, even though now they use plastic or nylon or whatever. But if I see a cat, I think of violins. Violins. Violence.

I don't know what happened to Mr. Raisin and his cats and violin because we moved when I was six. And I missed him. But moving when you're six is something you can't do anything about. It just happens, your parents decide to move, and that's that.

Life seems to be pretty much full of stuff you can't do anything about. For instants, I had this dog whose name was Kelly. He was shaggy and he had these bangs covering his eyes like some people I know. We had just moved to a house with a yard and Dad got him so I'd have a playmate which was great, especially since I don't have any brothers or sisters. Me and Kelly had a great time. He was such a stupid dog and did really disgusting things like eat his own barf and stuff like that, but I really liked him anyway because of the way he used to look at me, like, "What are we going to do next? Huh? Huh?"

He was always ready to play. Always. The only thing was I felt sorry for him because I thought he couldn't see for all that hair in his eyes. So I cut it. What I didn't know is that dogs who have hair covering their eyes have that hair because they are bred that way. In fact, if they don't have that hair covering their eyes they can get infections and stuff which will make them go blind. Which is exactly what happened to Kelly.

First he got sores in his eyes and they were full of pus, then he wandered out onto the street to follow me when I left the gate open, and I watched him get hit by a car. The driver didn't even stop.

All my fault. I did it all. I killed him.

My Dad buried him in the backyard. But before he put him in the hole, he asked me if I wanted to say good-bye to him, like there was nothing wrong, like he was just going away for awhile. And Kelly was lying there just as if he was asleep, but there were flies on his blind eyes and he was dead and I killed him.

So big deal, right? A dead dog. Everybody has their dead dog story. It's a dumb thing to talk about and I don't even know why I did, except for some reason it was on my mind. How you can go from a piano to a dead dog beats me. But while I'm on the subject of animals, there's one more little story I got to tell about when I was little. It's about a buffalo.

It was a couple years after Kelly and on TV they were showing these buffalo (okay, I know it's *bison*, but I like buffalo better) that they were moving from someplace north to a park down south. It was, like, quite a haul from one end of the province to the other. Anyway, they were showing these trucks with buffalo getting out of them and going into these pens. And one of the buffalo gets all excited and he jumps out of the pen and starts running, and everyone is chasing after him. But the old buffalo gets away. They can't catch him. And before they know it, he's gone, he's history.

Anyway, I'm cheering for the buffalo, and all my little buddies in grade three or four are cheering for him too. And every now and then, there'd be a report that this buffalo had been seen someplace, mixed in with some cows making beefalos, I guess, and then he'd disappear again. And we'd cheer again, amazed that all these adults with trucks and planes couldn't catch this buffalo.

This went on for a couple of months, people seeing the buffalo, and him disappearing. And all the while he was heading in a certain direction. North. He was going back home. And if you remember the story yourself, you know what happened, he made it. He actually made it without being caught, from one end of the province to the other.

And when he got there, this one lonely old buffalo, what did they do? They didn't have a party or some kind of celebration, no. They shot him. They put a bullet through his heart.

I tell you what, they might as well have shot me too.

But they didn't shoot me and I'm a big target, just about six feet with blond hair and blue eyes. Sometimes I get called Jaw, because I have one that tends to stick out a bit. Or maybe it's because I talk a lot. Anyway, there's still hope I'm going to make it home without getting shot. The only problem is I don't know what home is. I mean, yeah, it's the place you keep your pillow and eat your breakfast, but what is it really?

All right, who in their right minds thinks about stuff like this? I mean, you would have to be slightly out of your mind to even bother. Which I suppose goes to prove that I am slightly out of my mind. I mean, you'd never guess, but normally I would prefer to think about other things, like hockey, and here I start off telling you about how neat a piano is, and that, like, it's like some kind of miracle. Then I get sidetracked into talking about dead animals, which makes no sense unless you understand I'm trying to figure out why I took it up — playing piano. It seems like I didn't have a whole lot of choice. It was either that or take up talking to plants in a major way, or committing murder or several other things that are quite dangerous to your health. It's amazing what stress will do to the human mind.

Chapter two

It's a long story. I'll tell it like it is. It starts with hockey. I mean, hockey isn't everything. It's just a game. But it's a game I've played since I was six, where I'm in charge and no one else. I love it because every now and then, when it all comes together and you do it right, it can make you feel like God. Not that I know what God feels like. I mean, I'm taking a wild guess at what he might feel like, if in fact he feels anything at all, which occasionally I have my doubts about. And what do I know? I'm only fifteen — something my parents keep reminding me of — in my first year of Junior B, in a half-decent league, the kind the scouts check out from time to time.

If you were going to hear the coach talk about me, he'd say, "He's got good size, a bit of speed, and he keeps his head up," all of which is a compliment. It's the kind of thing you'd like to hear the scouts say about you. It's like a big fantasy to make the NHL. But I'm not holding my breath. Chances are, like, one in a thousand to even get drafted. Scouts are these guys who work for NHL teams. They're looking for prospects. They have notebooks and make notes on players they see. You hardly ever notice them. They specialize in being invisible.

But mostly I just love the game. Tonight we're playing the Mohawks. We're one, one and one with them so far this year. It can't get much more even, even though we play totally different styles. We move the puck and skate, the whole team. They're a bunch of goons with a couple of snipers.

It's late in the game and as usual we're tied. We're in our end at the blue line, and this stupid frigging goon about six foot three who's clubbed me at least twice on the back of the head, winds up and he's going to take the biggest slapshot of his life, while I coast at him with my legs together not wanting to damage the plumbing. He brings his stick from way over his head down through the puck and he's got everything behind it. If he gets all of it, it's going right through me. It's funny how it seems to happen in slow motion. The puck rises a black blur and catches me square in the left thigh pad. I don't feel a thing. It doesn't go through me. In fact, it bounces off me a couple meters past him. The goon jabs his stick between my legs, off-balance. I hop. Down he goes. I'm on my way, alone. A breakaway!

I'm full stride wide open. The puck hits snow. I lose it off my stick but kick it with my skate in front of me. To their blue line. Their goalie is coming way out.

I shift left, then right.

He follows.

Quick left again.

He's down!

I back-hand it high into the middle of the net.

It's a thing of beauty, it really is. I feel like God and pile full tilt into the net.

As I get untangled, our guys skate up to me and bang me with their sticks, and generally give me a good friendly roughing up. If this was the other team doing that, the gloves would be off by now.

"Nice play!"

"Way to go, Jaw." And that sort of thing. I'm feeling pretty good. I notice the goon smashes his stick against the boards. It doesn't break. He wanted to break it. Can't blame his stick.

I skate back to the bench while the announcer says, "Breaker's goal scored by number eighty-nine, Lanny Reich, unassisted." There's a few fans there, mostly family and stuff. They cheer. I see Dad. His fist shaking in the air and a silly grin sneaking out from behind his beard. And Mom beside him, clapping like an idiot, a cigarette in her hand. She's going to hit the guy next to her in the eyeball. I notice he's worried about it too. He moves a bit. And takes out a notebook. A scout!

Chapter Three

After the game I ask my Mom what the guy was writing in his notebook. She says, "What guy?"

I say, "The guy next to you."

"That was your father," she says.

"On the other side — the scout," I say.

And she says, "I never noticed anyone next to me."

I swear to God, scouts are invisible. Or maybe they're only visible to earthlings.

I have this theory that parents are from another planet. Someplace far away and long ago. The proof is this: look in their eyes. See anything there? Nothing. Nothing but great vast tracks of space. They look at you with those great vast tracks of space-eyes, and they're thinking thoughts from another planet. Their mouths open and sounds come out. "Take out the garbage. Clean your room." They make marks on pieces of paper, notes, and leave them lying around, "Supper's in the microwave. Pick you up after practice." I mean whose idea was parents anyway? Not mine. And you don't even get to choose them. They're just there. Pot luck. The two of them hit the hay some night, and lo and behold! We spring from their loins! Spacey. How alien can you get?

So, you'd think we'd live in a space ship, right? Wrong. We live in one of those places that if you look in the Real Estate section of the paper, they call a Character Home. That means it's old. It's got wood all over the place that people forgot to paint. And if they didn't forget, then you're supposed to scrape it off to match the other stuff. Personally, I've got nothing against paint. I think it can cover up a lot of garbage. But Mom and Dad really like wood. So this place has more wood than you can shake a stick at. It's got rooms all over the place that make you feel like you're living in a maze. Shawna, a friend of mine, said that. She said, "This place is *amazing.*" She was just stating facts. Consequently, Dad is constantly knocking out walls to make the place look bigger and take out that "amazing" feeling. And you got to put up with all this chalk dust all over the place. It gets in your hair and up your nose. The place is always full of paint and wallpaper. It's got oak floors that slope in a couple directions. Drop a marble, and you never know where it's going to go. They sanded them down and urethaned them last summer. The place stank for weeks. And it still didn't stop the creaking. Every time you move, it sounds like something's going to cave in. Oh yeah, and the windows leak.

The wind comes up and it feels like you're sitting in the middle of a ball park. Every fall Dad's there with rolls of plastic and a staple gun trying to cut down the wind. The only neat thing about a Character Home is that it's got a fireplace. In the winter, which is most of the time here, Dad gets to burn the inside of the walls he's torn down. It's great, especially if you don't mind the smoke that belches back at you every now and then.

And then there's my room.

I live in the basement. After Dad knocked out a couple dozen walls upstairs, we were short of rooms. So he built me one in the basement. This room has no wood in it. It's great. Sort of L-shaped with a couch, a waterbed, and my ghetto, and lots of wall space for hanging posters and stuff. But I keep one wall clear. Blank. I like a blank wall to stare at from time to time. Because next to it I've got autographed pictures of Paul Coffey when he played with the Oilers, Wendel Clark (my personal idol), Ray Bourque, and a friend of a friend who plays for Pittsburgh but mostly sits on the bench, Jerry Adams. I also got pictures of Alannah Myles, who I wouldn't kick out of bed for eating crackers, and a bunch of people you probably never heard of because they're old, like the Beatles, Paul McCartney's old band. The only reason I have them is because my Dad and Mom gave them to me. One of them I actually like, Minglewood. That guy is so cool. He sings the blues. I play that tape a lot, even though none of my friends know who he is. He's one of those guys who survived the sixties, which goes to show good things can survive. I mean, look at my parents. Even though they're aliens, I admit they're neat. Weird, but neat.

Okay, so let me introduce you. First, but for no particular reason, my father the poet. Great.

"Hey Jaw, what does your Dad do?" I mean, every now and then the question comes up, and what do you say?

"He aah . . . " and I stall.

"Well, what does he do? Rob banks?"

"I wish."

"No really, what does he do?"

"He writes."

"Oh yeah? Like what?"

And this is where it gets embarrassing.

"He just writes stuff."

"Like what? For newspapers?"

You know, you'd think I'd learn to lie about it. But by now they're suspicious. They know I'm trying to hide something.

"He's a poet."

"A what!?"

"A poet. He writes poems."

"Holy shit. Did you guys hear that?"

And it goes downhill from there. I don't dare mention that he cooks too. I don't mean like the barbecue steaks, I'm talking garbanzo bean chili. And lentils. Does anybody in this day and age know what a lentil is? It's a little flat bean that gags anybody under the age of forty. That's how old he is, my father the poet.

And listen, my mother is a saint. She is a social worker. She has all these clients that are poor and depressed. She gets mad when the government cuts programs that help people. She really is like one of these old saints who go around doing good for people all day long, except she doesn't brag about it. So no one's going to name a church after her or anything. She is also into fitness. She runs five miles a day. The funny thing is she smokes like a forest fire. I'm talking moochos cigarettos. She smokes more than my science teacher (Mr. Mooney, great name, eh) and he's constantly in the john lighting up. He can't even get through a class without disappearing for his nicotine fix. Great role models. And I'm not supposed to notice any of this. Guess what, guys, I notice.

Anyway, the assumption is parents are from another planet. And they don't know which planet but as soon as they find out we're going to send them all back. I'm on the Help-Your-Parents-Find-Their-Planet committee at school. You can send your donations to me. It's not really a committee, it's just a joke, but a bunch of us sit around and tell stories about how screwed up our parents are. Actually, I'm in pretty good shape really. Some of the kids don't have parents, or don't have the regular number. They either have one, or about six. Shawna's got about six. She's got different parents for weekends, for Christmas, for practically every season of the year. I don't know how she can sort it out. I got enough trouble with two. She thought that "springing from your loins" phrase was pretty funny. She went, "Boing, boing, boing", and laughed till she cried. It does make you laugh. Or cry. Or both I guess.

Take my parents, for instants. (I know it's supposed to be "for instance", but Shawna writes it like "instants" and I kind of like it better. I like her too. She got me to write this story, so any time you see me use the wrong words the right way, she and you can pick them out.) Anyway, take my parents for instants. (My mother hates it when I repeat myself.) My father the poet and my mother the saint are two perfectly normal-looking human beings — on the outside. On the inside, who knows. Dad sits in front of a typewriter all day, except when he's cooking or giving readings or going to meetings, and Mom's out smoking and saving the world. They have this thing about being open and honest. You have to talk all the time about

22 YULETIDE BLUES

everything you do. I mean, there are times when you just don't feel like talking. So consequently, they think I'm not being open and honest. They think I'm hiding something. What's there to hide? Consequently, they don't trust me. Which is just fine with me, because I don't trust them either — only I have a good reason for it. And I'll tell you about it in a minute.

You can always tell it's going to be an openness and honesty session when my father the poet starts with something like:

"Listen, your mother and I have been talking . . . "

I mean, really, break that down. The first word he uses is "listen", which means he's going to do the talking and I'm going to do the listening. Then he says, "your mother and I." This is his subtle way of including me in the family by admitting I have a mother. I mean, he could say, "my wife and I" or "Colleen and I", but no, it's my mother, the one who went through all the pain and agony giving birth to me, springing from the loins. And finally, "have been talking". I'm good at grammar, "have been", past tense. Need I say more? It's a fate accomplea. So, okay, we're being open and honest here.

But I've got to paint the whole picture. These open and honest sessions always take place in the kitchen. "Come in here and sit down." That means sit down at the kitchen table. It's a wood table, an antique. Mom bought it at an auction. She paid a hundred and eighty-nine bucks for it, the price of a decent SunIce. The only problem with it, is that it only had three legs. So Dad made the fourth. He did a pretty good job. It looks just like the other three, except for the colour of the wood. But that's fine. The chairs they got later match the one leg great. They're supposed to be antiques too. But if they're such great antiques, howcome they don't match the rest of the old table? I guess they're the kind of things our grandparents used to sit on all the time. They'll kill you if you sit on them too long. No wonder they invented plastic and foam, anything to get off those old wooden chairs. Don't tell them I said so, but I think they are not only uncomfortable, they look dorky too.

Anyway, I'm now sitting there at the kitchen table, nearest the odd-coloured leg, and I admit it, I got some annoying habits. One of them is this: no matter how hard I try, I always manage to spill some milk when I'm pouring it into a glass. Then I kind of, like, make designs with the little bit I've spilled — sort of spread it out, doodle with it. This bugs my mother no end. She says, "Stop playing with your milk. Wipe it up." Dad never says anything. He's secretly hoping I'll be an artist. He doesn't want to stifle me. And tonight, someone has forgot to wipe the table after supper. (Me.) And there's a bit of milk on it where I sit, as per usual. Of course, I start to doodle with it.

"Stop playing with your milk. Wipe it up," says Mom, as she casually lights up one of her cancer sticks. I don't say anything. I get up and go to the sink and get a J-cloth. I come back and wipe it up. I throw it back to the sink for two points, banking it off the faucet.

"Nice shot," Dad says. "Listen, your mother and I have been talking. We want to go someplace warm for a couple of weeks over Christmas — ten days, to be exact."

At this point, really, I am thinking, "Great, fantastic!" Then he lowers the boom.

"The only problem is, what to do with you."

I already know that I am doomed, that if what-to-do-with-me is a *problem*, that I'm not included in this deal, but hey, I'm being open and honest. Two can play this game. So I say, "What do you mean?"

This puts my mother the Social Worker into gear. She says, "Well, we can't leave you alone."

Now I think, "Oh God, I'm going to stay at the grandparents'?" I have both sets. I mean, if parents are from another planet, grandparents are from another universe — an old universe. They don't even have cable TV. They have antennas sticking out of their roofs, something you hardly see anymore. Watching TV there is like watching a snowstorm. But Mom continues.

"Your grandparents have offered . . . "

They've even told them without telling me.

". . . but your grandpa could go in for his knee operation at any time and so that might be awkward. . . Blah, blah, blah . . . "

You want to know what the aliens have done behind my back? They have planned a winter holiday! I mean they have planned a couple weeks lying around on some beach somewhere, living in a beer commercial in the middle of winter, while I stay home alone and freeze my butt off!

Now it might not be any great revelation to you, but it comes as quite a shock to me that life is not fair. I mean why should the aliens get to go someplace warm, while we earth creatures, the only ones who are truly able to appreciate this planet, who have the ability to see scouts, are stuck here in the vast reaches of frozen snow? It is so cold here that my father the poet's beard freezes to his mustache when he goes out to try and get the car going. Of course, half the time it doesn't start, and in he comes swearing about how cold it is, and you can't make out what he's saying because his mouth is frozen shut. I kind of get a charge out of it and almost suspect him of being human, but that's how cold it is, I kid you not.

And you know, to be perfectly honest about it, that's not what really bugs me — I mean the fact that I'm not going — what really bugs me is the open and honest way they told me they were going. The way it's all stacked against me. The way I'm left without anything to really say about it. Except where I'm going to stay.

My mother takes another drag from her cancer stick.

"And so we were wondering if you have any suggestions."

"Take me along!" I mean, that's my first suggestion. There's no harm in running it up the flag-pole to see who salutes.

"No," my father the poet says. He can be really precise sometimes.

"What do you mean?" I say.

"Well, we just want to go alone. And I don't think we could afford it either."

This is where I dig in.

"Aah," I say. I turn it up at the end, to show I'm really disappointed. I think my voice even cracks. Mother's turn.

"You've been with us on every vacation we've ever had. We want to go on one alone. And what about your hockey? You'd miss four games."

I do some quick calculating. "Two weeks!? You're going for *two weeks*?" It occurs to me. "Where you going?"

"Dominican Republic," Dad says.

"And you'd miss at least four practices too." Mom always seems to be a step behind.

"Mom, I don't care. Dominican Republic? Where's that?"

"It's in the Caribbean, beside Cuba."

"Isn't there a revolution there or something?" I say, flailing in the dark.

"Yes, there was. In 1965," Dad says. He'd know too. It's in the sixties, his specialty. He's twisting his beard with his finger, twirling little curls. I shift my weight in the chair. The floor creaks. I wish it would cave in. There is at this moment something that someone once called a pregnant pause. It's one of those pauses that is about to give birth to something. My mother drags on her cancer stick and knocks a bit of ash into the ashtray. It occurs to me that I should do what a friend of a friend of Jerry Adams did once. I do it. I stick my index finger in the bottom of the ashtray, give it a scrape, bring it to my tongue and lick it.

"Lanny! How can you be so gross!" Mom. Almost jumping.

"It's only on my tongue, not in my lungs," I offer, pithily.

"We're waiting for some suggestion, Lanny. What do you want to do?" Dad says.

"Well, how do I know? What am I supposed to do? You guys are planning to go away and you don't want me along. I'm supposed to figure out what to do with myself? I'll stay home."

"We can't let you stay home by yourself. You're only fifteen." That's Mom. Age is very important to Mom.

"So if I'm too young to stay home alone, then I should come along." Sometimes my logic overwhelms me. It doesn't have any effect on them though. They've got their own logic.

"If you're too young to stay home alone, then someone's got to stay with you." Dad's logic.

"Well, who then?"

"We don't know. That's why we're asking if you have any suggestions." Mom again.

"I don't know!" I get up and go to the fridge. I open it up and stare inside. Nothing. Well, nothing interesting. "Howcome this is always empty?"

"Because you always empty it."

He's right. I do. I eat a lot. I take out the milk. And close the door. I get a glass out of the dishrack and pour. Over the sink. As per usual, I spill some. "You still haven't said why I can't come along."

Mom sucks smoke. "We've given you three reasons. First, we want to go alone, we've never *had* a vacation alone . . . "

"What about before I was born?" I interrupt, knowing I've got something there.

"That was sixteen years ago."

"I haven't had a vacation alone for sixteen years either."

"Well, then you know what we mean," Dad says.

And Mom continues, "Secondly, you'll miss all that hockey."

"I don't care."

"Your coach does. Your team will. There's sixteen guys depending on you. It's a commitment you made. Not to mention that you already paid for it — *we* paid for it." My Dad talks like that. Complete sentences. He's probably a good poet too.

"And third, we can't afford it." Mom is a bottom-liner. She should have been an accountant.

"Yeah, we really can't afford it," echoes Dad. It's not like Dad to echo. It really must be the bottom line. I see a glimmer of light way at the end of the tunnel.

"How much would it cost?"

"Would what cost?"

See?! I've caught Mom off guard!

"To take me along, how much would it cost?"

"About a thousand bucks." Dad was too quick on that. You can shift and deke, but you can't fool the old poet.

30 YULETIDE BLUES

"A thousand!? A thousand dollars?" That's what a friend of a friend of Jerry Adams paid for his car. He's sixteen. His old man sells them, cars. I get lost for a moment in cars and take a drink of milk. I dribble and wipe my mouth with my sleeve. Then, suddenly, it dawns on me.

"If I raise a thousand dollars can I go?"

"Where are you going to get a thousand dollars?" Mom asks.

"I don't know, but if I get it can I go too?"

"Sure. If you come up with a thousand bucks you can come. Or you could buy yourself a car for when you're sixteen. I don't care."

That's my father the poet. How did he know I was thinking about cars? He has this trick of knowing what I'm thinking. I have to come up with a trick of raising a thousand dollars.

Chapter four

We have this deal at our house. Actually it's not a deal, a deal involves two people. This only involves me, so it's a lousy deal. In order for me to play hockey, I have to take piano, as in piano lessons. I hate it, I resent it. I resent the music that I have to play. I resent the fact that my fingers can't ever hit the right keys. But most of all, I resent my piano teacher. And this is a problem because she's my aunt. Actually my great aunt, except I can't see what's so great about her. Technically she's my Dad's aunt, so that makes her my great aunt. Aunt Florence. She was born in Germany and came here after the Second World War and she still can't speak proper English. Her "w's" sound like "v's", and her "s's" either sound like "sh's" or hisses and she gets her grammar all garbled. The reason I have to take my lessons from her is because she gives Mom and Dad a break on the price she'd normally charge. I've been doing this for five years now and it's getting to the point where something unhealthy is going to happen, like murder or something. Every week we go through the same thing. She listens to me play and she shakes her head. "Vut iss dis?" she says,

"Vut iss dis?" And then she blithers on as to this and that and the other thing. I have no idea what she's talking about.

On top of that I have to practice a couple times a week at home. I get out of this fairly easy because no one ever comes into the "piano room" while I'm supposedly practicing, I doodle around a bit with stuff I like by Billy Joel or Elton John and then I put on this tape I made of me practicing Brahms or Beethoven, two dead guys, and crank it up through the stereo which is in the same room. Then I read or something with my Walkman on. One of these days I'm going to get caught, but who cares.

So this is where I am now, listening to *Minglewood*. Mat Minglewood. I don't know why I like him. He plays kind of rock and roll blues, but if you listen really carefully, you can almost hear bagpipes too. I like the bagpipes. Scottish, like my Mom. It's the only instrument I know that can wake you up and put you to sleep at the same time, soothing and rousing together at once. When you think of music in German, my Dad's side of the family, the Reich side, all you can think of is oom-pa-pa beer-swilling guys in leather shorts. Or Aunt Florence going, "Vat iss diss?"

I've always been a bit embarrassed by my name Reich. Supposedly it means "rich". I don't know why they don't just translate it, drop the "e" and have a name that everyone can understand. In all the old war movies the bad guys are always the Germans. I mean today in real life it's Iraqis but it used to be Germans. Think what it would be like to have an Iraqi name, Abdul or something, Saddam. No picnic, I tell you living with a name like Saddam. I used to get called a "squarehead kraut". I can thank my Dad for that, for not changing our name. He has this thing, you should be proud of your heritage. Yeah, maybe, but not when it means you get dumped on just for having a name.

All this stuff is running through my mind for no particular reason, except that one thing leads to another, and suddenly I realize somebody is tapping me on the shoulder. I look up.

"Hi Dad."

"You're not practicing."

I knew I'd get caught sooner or later. I didn't think it would be this soon.

"We had an agreement," he says.

"What?"

"You know."

"I never agreed to the agreement. *You* had an agreement."

"No practice, no hockey," he says. "Come on, get to it."

I take off my headphones and look him in the eye.

"Why do I have to do this?"

"You don't *have* to do anything."

"Yes I do. If I don't do this I can't play hockey."

"You answered your own question."

"Yeah but why? Why can't I do something I want to do, without having to do something I don't want to do?"

"Because life's like that."

I hate that answer, life's like that. It's so encouraging. Howcome *his* life isn't like that?

"Oh yeah? You only do what you want to do."

"You think so, do you."

"You're going on a trip. You do whatever you want."

"There's a lot of things I don't want to do."

"Like what?"

"Like making you practice the piano."

"Well, if you don't like making me practice, and I don't want to practice, howcome I'm practicing?"

"Because you want to play hockey."

This doesn't make any sense. I've been buffaloed. I now have a clearer idea of where that saying came from. Being buffaloed.

"I want to go to the Caribbean with you."

"You can't."

"Why not?"

"We've been through this, Lanny."

"See, you do whatever you want."

"Practice your piano."
"Why?!"
"Because I said so."

This is the bottom line. *Because he said so.* He turns and leaves the room. I know he means it. I climb onto the piano stool and start banging disgustedly on the keys. This is about as much fun as growing rocks. Maybe I've lost the battle, but the war is on.

CHAPTER FIVE

It's after practice, *hockey* practice, and a couple of us are hanging out around the canteen having a Coke. There's Boog and me and a friend of a friend of Jerry Adams whose real name is Dozen. Well, I mean, guys call him Dozen because his *real* name is Egbert or something like that and we called him Eggie for awhile but he always has so much stuff that it gradually got changed to Dozen, as in a dozen eggs. Both of them are pretty good guys and we hang out a lot together, except that Boog has some of the absolute worst personal habits, as befits his name, which is really short for "booger". *His* real name is Michael, although I don't think I've ever heard anyone ever call him that. If there was one change he could make in his life, it would be that people would call him Michael. And everyone knows that. Consequently, everyone calls him Boog.

"Boog, would you stop snaking your nose. You're going to make me barf," says Dozen.

"Well then, lend me your hanky," says Boog. This is not an unreasonable request, since Dozen is the only guy we know who actually carries one.

"Forget it. I don't want your snot all over my hanky. Go get some toilet paper or something."

"Door's locked," says Boog. It is too. The guy who runs the rink always locks it so you have to go see him for a key. That way he can keep track of who's wrecking it. Except it keeps getting wrecked anyway. I have no idea who does it. It wouldn't surprise me if it was Boog though.

"Hey, Boog," I say, "Are you the guy who keeps stuffing toilet paper into the john?"

"Me?" he says. "No, why would I do that?"

"Why do you pick your nose?" I ask.

Boog squeezes his Coke and shoots a gob of it on me. I sidestep. It hits Dozen. Of course Dozen is real pleased. Both me and Boog laugh, but it's not that funny. I mean, Dozen usually wears pretty good clothes. To show he's not a complete jerk, Boog gets some napkins from the canteen and helps Doze wipe his jacket. Except he more or less rubs it in deeper.

Opposite the canteen is a big window facing the parking lot. It must be made of some high-tech glass, the kind of stuff they use in the space shuttle or something. I've seen guys take some pretty good shots at it, seriously, and nothing happens.

We drift over to the window sort of half-dragging, half-carrying our bags with us. Because it's dark outside, you can mostly see our reflection in the window. You have to get pretty close to it before you can see outside. Boog is waiting for a ride from his Dad, or Mom or someone. Dozen's car is on the fritz so his Dad is coming to get him. I just live around the corner. I get to walk.

Dozen would probably be playing Junior A if he wasn't so small. He says he's going to work on his body so he can make Junior A next year. He might do it too. He says his great-great-great-grandmother was a Cree Indian and that gives him inner strength. And even though he's got these high cheek-bones and sort of almond eyes, he also has red hair and freckles. I don't know. He's also got a bit of a chip on his shoulder and I wonder about his moods sometimes. He can go for days without saying boo to his own shadow, then all of a sudden everything's hunky-dory and you really don't know what's going on with him. It might have something to do with the fact that he lives alone with his Dad and doesn't get to see his Mom because she lives in Vancouver. But I really don't know because he never talks about it much, except in a kind of joking way. But one thing's for sure, he's smarter than most guys. And I like him. For a guy who's got money coming out his ears, he's really quite generous. He'll give you the shirt off his back, which in my case wouldn't mean much because it'd be too small. But, for instants, I'm sure he'll lend me his car when I turn sixteen.

Boog's our goalie. He's good. He's very good. He's going to make the NHL sometime, and what's really neat about Boog is that he doesn't know how good he is. He is also very handsome. I hate to use the word, but that's what he is. You have this image of goalies always being ugly guys with their noses hanging out. Not Boog. If you were going to cast him in a movie or something, you'd have to get Tom Cruise. That's who he looks like. But he makes up for it by being a complete slob. You've never met such a slob. And awkward. On the ice, he's like a Russian ballet dancer, but off, he's El Klutzo. He'd trip over his own shadow. You still can't help but like the guy, in spite of himself.

We sit on our bags and stare at ourselves, pretending we're looking out the window. All of a sudden Dozen looks harder. He sees something across the parking lot. Me and Boog notice him looking and we look too. It's a girl, or a woman, jogging on the other side of the street.

"I think I should take up jogging," says Dozen.

"I wouldn't kick her out of bed for eating crackers," says Boog. Doze and I both look at him. Boog is an avowed and notorious virgin. I mean, most of us are, but him even more so. He is terrified of girls. That's why they like him so much. That and the fact he looks like Tom Cruise. We turn back to the window.

"Yeah, she's not bad," I say. As these words leave my lips, the woman passes under the street light at the end of the parking lot.

I recognize who it is. "Holy shit!"

"You know her?" says Dozen.

"It's my Mom!" They just about die laughing. I fail to see the humour of the situation. Lusting after my own mother. Frankly, it's disgusting.

"I don't see what's so funny, you guys," I say.

"It's not," says Dozen, "It's the way you said it." He bursts into another fit of merry yucks.

"'Holy shit, it's my Mom!'" says Boog, joining him, slipping off onto the floor. He is on his back, doubled up.

"Aw, come on," I say. "It's not that funny." I am looking desperately for ways of changing the subject. An earthquake would help. A loonie slides out of Boog's pocket, a loonie then twenty-five cents. I pounce on it.

"Hey, that's mine," says Boog.

"I charge a buck and a quarter for laughs like that," I say. "Come on, Doze, you owe me a buck and a quarter."

"Sure," he says, meaning "stuff it".

"In fact," I say, "I need another thousand of these."

"That's a lot of laughs," says Boog.

"No, really, I need a thousand dollars," I say.

"What for?" says Dozen. Money is no laughing matter to him. Mention a thousand dollars, and he gets serious right away.

I give Boog back his money. "To go to the Caribbean."

"Oh sure, me too," says Boog.

"Are you serious?" asks Dozen.

"Yeah, my parents are going. And if I want to go, I have to raise a thousand bucks." As I say this, I realize that it sounds a little more weird than it really is.

"That's weird," says Boog. "You mean they're just going to leave you here if you can't raise it?"

"Yeah, well I mean they're not going to *abandon* me or anything. I'll stay at my grandparents' or someplace." I suddenly get spooked at the thought of "someplace". I know my grandparents are busy or having operations and stuff, and very briefly the thought of "someplace" puts Aunt Florence in mind. She flits across it for just a second. I quickly get rid of her. "But if I raise a thousand dollars, I can go too."

"How can you raise a thousand bucks?" asks Dozen. If there's a way, he'd like to know about it.

"I don't know. It's a lot of money," I say.

"You're telling me. I can't raise one-sixty for a new starter," says Dozen. We both look at him.

"Dad said he'd buy the car, but I'd have to maintain it." We all stare at ourselves in the window again.

"You know what Jerry Adams drives?" says Dozen. He has a friend who is a friend of Jerry Adams.

"What?" says Boog.

"A Porsche."

"I thought he was just sitting on the bench," says Boog.

"He is," says Dozen.

"Wow," says Boog. His finger goes to his nose. But he scratches it instead. "I saved a hundred bucks for my new pads." Doze and I look at Boog. "It took me three years."

I don't have three years. I don't have three months.

It isn't long before Dozen's Dad pulls up in what looks like a luxury liner, the Queen Mary or something, minus the fog-horn. Boog's Mom shows up after that in what might be the fog-horn missing on Dozen's Dad's car. It is amazingly ugly, but Boog's Mom isn't bad looking, I mean, for a mother.

I drag my stuff home and hang it in the basement so it dries out and doesn't grow strange things like it does when you leave it in the bag too long. I go upstairs and meet Mom coming out of the shower. For some reason I'm a little embarrassed seeing her like this, I mean, even though she is covered in towels and stuff.

"Hi, how was your practice?" she says, rubbing a corner of the towel through her hair and walking to her room. The floor is going to cave in any minute now. I can't believe how it creaks.

"Not bad," I say, going to the fridge to look for something to eat. "Where's the poet?" I ask.

"At a meeting, I guess," she hollers from their room.

I grab a loaf of bread and the peanut butter. And a carton of milk. We get that health food peanut butter where all the oil floats to the top. You've got to stir it in when you get it and then put it in the fridge so it stays mixed up. "Saw you jogging by the rink."

"Oh yeah?" She's proud of the fact she jogs.

"Boog said he wouldn't kick you out of bed for eating crackers." I'm not sure why I say this, but I do.

"He said what?!" says Mom, appearing at the door with a very quizzical look on her face.

"He didn't know it was you, *I* didn't know it was you — till later, after you got under the light."

"Oh." She turns away and disappears back into their room. She's probably trying to decide whether to be concerned or to be flattered.

I plaster the bread with peanut butter and attempt, yet again, to pour milk without spilling.

No go. This is amazing. Why can't I do this? Sometimes I think I'm suffering from a strange disease. It's only three drops. I join them together making a little triangle and take a bite of the sandwich. "How'm I going to raiph a thouphan' darphs?"

"What? Don't talk with your mouth full."

I take a drink of milk. "How am I going to raise a thousand dollars?"

"I don't know. That's your problem." This from a woman whose business it is to console others.

"Mother, don't you care about me, your son, the fruit of your loins."

"Lanny, don't talk like that."

"Sorre-e-e!" Sometimes she doesn't like my humour.

"Have you thought about Aunt Florence?" Now that's funny. Ha ha ha. I just about choke.

"Mother, I would rather be dead. I would rather be dead and living in hell than stay with Aunt Florence."

"I wouldn't say that if I were you," she says, emerging. "All freshly bathed and scented, feeling like a brand new human being." She always says that after a shower. It's a line from a play by some guy whose name begins with a state, Kentucky or something. She told me once, but I forget.

"It's a definite possibility," she continues, "Especially now."

"What do you mean, 'especially now'?"

"Well, now that she's in a wheelchair."

"Oh God." Life is rapidly becoming not worth living, if this is what I've got to look forward to.

"On the other hand, I wonder what Daphne's doing?"

And here I really do choke. "Aunt Daphy?"

"The peanut butter reminded me of her," Mom says.

You have to know Aunt Daphne. She lives on nuts and berries and that sort of thing. She's Dad's sister. I call her Aunt Daphy. I like her a lot. But boy, is she weird. Mom used to call her "Day-glo". Dad still does. That's because when the sixties moved on into the seventies (when I was born) Aunt Daphne didn't come along. She stayed there. She is a living museum of the sixties. She wears tie-dyed skirts, and a head band keeps her long blonde hair out of her eyes, which are always squinty like the sun's too bright. She says, "oh wow", and "too much". She makes beautiful delicate pottery and jewelry out of porcelain that are just like her. Except for her hands. She has the hands of a butcher. I mean, she has big meaty hands. When I was little, she used to let me make things out of clay that always turned into ashtrays. Consequently, our place is littered with these dumb-looking ashtrays I made when I was a kid. Maybe that's why Mom smokes. She feels she has to use these things. But I tell you what, spending a couple weeks with weird Aunt Daphne would be really neat. The only trouble is nobody ever knows where she is. She travels a lot.

"I wonder if she's home?" Mom says. "Where's my purse?" There's actually a connection here. Mom keeps a little phone number book in her purse. But she can never find it. In order to find Aunt Daphne, we've got to find Mom's purse first. No problem. It's behind me, hung over the chair.

"Here it is." I hand it to her. While she's looking up the number she says, "You wouldn't mind staying with her, would you?"

"Oh no," I say, "That'd be great." And it would be. It'd be an adventure. "I could make more ashtrays."

Mom looks at me, trying to decide if that was a joke or not.

"It's a joke," I say.

"Good," she says, going to the phone, "I wish I could quit too."

Telepathy. They can read your mind, parents/aliens. Maybe it just comes with age. Aunt Daphy reads teacups. You have a cup of tea but you don't use teabags, just the leaves floating around in your cup and sticking in your teeth. Then when they settle to the bottom, after you've drank most of it, she reads the design they make, sort of like how a quarterback reads the defence. At least that's what she told me. When she travels, she goes to these psychic conventions, you know, like "Friends of the Universe" and that kind of thing. She has this theory that hockey is a ritualized form of intergalactic combat and that Wayne Gretzky comes from the planet Zulon and he was sent here to raise our consciousness. But she'll tell you this stuff with a little smirk on her face, so you really have no idea if she means it or not. She also knows more about hockey than anybody alive. She even knows who Jerry Adams is.

Mom reads me Aunt Daph's phone number and I dial. It's a habit we got into. She taught me numbers this way when I was about two. Anyway, Aunt Daphy doesn't answer, but her answering machine does. It starts with the sound of breaking glass. "Hi," the machine says, "sorry I can't come to the phone right now. I'm cleaning up some broken glass, or maybe I'm in the bathroom or somewhere else on the planet or universe. Anyway, please leave your name or the name of your travel agent and I'll get back to you as soon as I can. Bye. Oh, you might as well leave your phone number too so I can call."

Chapter six

There's five of us who hang out together. Me, Dozen and Boog are the guys, which I guess you can figure out. And then there's Shawna and Maureen. Let me tell you about them.

First Maureen. Maureen's got these eyes that'll look right through you. Even in her school photo her eyes do that. They're brown, the colour of that really good chocolate. They make her hair look blond, even though it isn't. Most people call her Moe but we call her Maureen and she likes that. You've got to agree with her most of the time, not because she's right, but because she'll break your arm if you don't. She's very strong. And very cheerful. She's got a smile that just lights up the room like a song. What I like most about her is she never wears make-up. She doesn't have to, but even lots of girls who don't have to *do*. And guys turn to look at her, her and those eyes. I think Boog has secret designs on Maureen. I mean they don't actually go out, but you can catch him looking at her from time to time with something other than brotherly affection if you get my drift.

Shawna. I got to admit, I probably look at Shawna the same way Boog looks at Maureen. Shawna has kind of frizzy blond hair. She is one of those people that no matter how you look at her, she always looks different. I think it has something to do with the soft angles her face has. She is also really tiny. And Dozen treats her like a little sister. He gives her rides and generally chauffeurs her around, when his car is working. But then her family life is pretty screwed up and I don't grudge anything Doze does for her. She's really tiny and wears clothes that make her blend into the walls and make her invisible. She'd make a good hockey scout. What I like most about Shawna is her voice. She has this great big gravelly voice that is totally unlike the rest of her and she uses it to say the most incredible things. She has what I call a beautiful mind. You never know where it's going to go, but wherever it is, you've never been there before. She plays with words all the time, like, "How come How come means How come?"

Anyway, the five of us hang out together at the mall. We bitch and complain about this and that, like for me it's about the piano and how I'm going to raise a thousand bucks. But mostly we just goof around during lunchtime when there's nothing to do at school. It's a great place to hang out, but if you ever want to shop there, forget it. Say you want something, a roll of hockey tape, and you go to the mall. Well as soon as you walk into the place your brain fries. It just goes blank. And you have to wander around looking at stuff for hours before you can remember what it is you came there for. And all these people are wandering around with the same kind of fried-brain look that you know you have. None of them knows why they're there. I don't know what it is. It must be the lights or something. I guess the theory is you'll wander around *buying* stuff till you *remember to buy* what you've come for, assuming of course that you've got enough money to do that. That's no problem for me because I never have any money. I guess that's one reason why it's a great place to hang out. You don't need money and your mind is gone. It gives you a great excuse to do stupid things.

For instants, as much complaining as I do about piano practice, I do like to horse around with it, the piano. There's a music store in the mall that sells mostly organs and occasionally we go in there where I noodle around doing my impression of Billy Joel. This lasts for about five minutes till the guy who owns the place figures we're scaring away business. Which is kind of a joke, because I've never actually seen anyone in there besides him. Anyway, that's an example of the kinds of things we do.

But mostly we either just walk around or we sit by the fountain where Boog fell in.

There's money in the fountain and it's just out of reach. Ask Boog. He'll tell you that reaching for money that's out of reach causes you to fall in — and then you feel like a real idiot going to school in wet clothes. Anyway, all five of us try to count it, which you can't because of the waves splashing from the water jet in the centre. There is also a blue balloon some little kid must have let go of that keeps getting dunked by the jet in the middle. It goes out a few feet then drifts back to the jet again. A very stupid balloon. It also doesn't help in counting the money.

"You guys are so stupid," says Maureen, "You can't *count* it. It's mostly pennies anyway."

"There's silver in there," says Boog.

"The question is," says Doze, "how did it get there?"

"People throw it there," says Boog.

"You?" asks Dozen.

"I don't *have* anything to throw away," says Boog.

"We *know* that," says Shawna.

"Well, neither do I," says Dozen, which is a flat out and out lie.

"You know," I say, "I've never actually *seen* anyone throw money in here."

"Neither have I," says Boog.

"I threw a penny in once," says Maureen, "when I was little, with my Dad."

"Okay, that accounts for one penny. There's hundreds in there," says Dozen.

"Thousands," says Boog.

"The question is not how much is there, but where does it go?" Shawna hits the nail on the pointy end and still drives it in.

"Yeah, where does it go?" I say.

"Forget it," Dozen says, "I know what you're thinking." He does too.

"I *need* it!" I say.

One of the things about raising a thousand bucks is that it's very hard to do. Although if there's a way, Dozen will figure it out.

"You're not going to get it stealing the pennies from the fountain," says Dozen. Then adds for Boog's sake, "Or the nickels or the dimes. You got to get a hold of something cheap and then sell it high."

"Like what, for instants?" says Shawna.

"Yeah, like what?" I say.

"Maureen's cheap, you could sell her," says Boog. This is not funny and Boog knows it. So does Maureen. She kicks him.

"Ow!" says Boog.

"Actually that's not that bad an idea. We could kidnap somebody and hold them for ransom," says Dozen.

Shawna turns sharply to Dozen and gives him a look I wouldn't want to sleep with. I don't know if he knows it but Shawna was kidnapped by one of her fathers when she was a kid. I don't think she thinks too much of kidnapping as an idea. But she says, "Sure, Dozen, we'll kidnap you. I'll bet we can get a thousand bucks for you."

"Yeah," says Boog, "actually we should go for two thousand. We'd have a thousand bucks left over."

"Why not five thousand," says Maureen, "then we could all go."

"We couldn't get five thousand for him," I say.

Right abouts now, Dozen is wishing he'd never opened his big mouth. "Okay! All right!" he says.

"How about Jerry Adams' Porsche?" says Boog, not giving up. "We could get five thousand for that."

"Who's Jerry Adams?" asks Maureen.

"What about your piano?" asks Dozen.

"What?" I say, as all forms of life freeze for a second.

"You hate that piano of yours so much, why don't you sell it?"

"Well for one thing, my parents would have something to say about it."

"So?"

"So what they would say is, like, forget it."

"Well, it's *yours*, isn't it?"

"Sort of."

"Didn't you say they gave it to you when you were ten?"

"Yeah, but . . . "

"And aren't you the only one who plays it?"

"Yeah."

"Well then, it's yours. Possession is nine-tenths of the law — technically it's yours," concludes Doze. If anyone should know about this, Doze should. His father sells cars.

But I'm still a little vague, "So?"

"So sell it! You could get a thou for it."

"I can't sell the piano!"

"Okay, it was just an idea," says Dozen.

Actually, as an idea, it's not bad. I just don't know how you could carry it out, either the idea *or* the piano. "How would you do it? I mean, what would you do?"

"Put an ad in paper," says Doze.

"Or have a garage sale," says Moe. "People will come flocking."

"A garage sale, get serious," says Boog.

"An ad in the paper," I say, warming to the idea.

"Actually, I know somebody who might be looking for a piano," says Shawna.

"Oh yeah, who?" I ask.

"Someone," says Shawna.

But we never find out who and forget about it in a hurry because the mall cop comes along to bitch at Boog for reaching into the fountain for coins. The mall cop tells us to get back to school.

CHAPTER SEVEN

It's the middle of Mr. Mooney's class. In fact it's the middle of one of his quizzes and he's ducked out for another nicotine fix. Talk about a creature of habit. Mr. Mooney always does things the same way. On Fridays we have quizzes. On Tuesdays we have little quizzes, or what he wittily calls "quizzicals". (Shawna wondered if he would call little tests "testicles.") He even sets up *before* class the same way. About five minutes to, he gets the overhead projector, plugs it in, puts his quiz questions on it, puts a piece of cardboard over to hide them, then he leaves for a quick smoke. Sometimes if we get there early, we take a peek at the questions, except that nobody can stand going to his class early, so we don't. But one of these days, it's going to get somebody into trouble.

Anyway, he's out of the class when Shawna passes me a note. The note says, "Call me after school."

I turn and nod to her, "yes," but as usual my timing is impeccable and Mr. Mooney enters and catches me mid-nod.

"Do you have something you'd like to share with the class, Mr. Reich?" he says.

This guy is trying to make me barf. I know he is.

"No," I say. But I know what's coming. He's going to say, "Well, you do now."

"Well, you do now," he says.

What this means is that after we mark this stupid quiz, the class will share my mark. It gets divided by the number of people in the class and split up. I get a share too. It's his lesson in socialism. Not that he's supposed to teach socialism, he's supposed to teach chemistry. He's probably very brilliant at it too. And why not, I mean, essentially chemicals are very stupid. You put them together and they always react the same way. Not like people. You put people together and you never know how they're going to react. But the guy couldn't teach his way out of a wet paper bag. I don't know why he teaches. He hates it. He hates kids. He should be golfing or jerking off or something. I hope I get about two percent. Let's see you guys share that. So far this is shaping up to be a pretty weird day. I should get Aunt Daphy to read my teacup. Except I hate tea.

* * *

"So how was your day," Dad says. He's putting water in a pot. Getting supper ready.

"Fine," I say. I don't know why I say that. It just comes out. The world could be ending and I'd still say "fine."

"Any homework?" he says.

"Nope," I say, opening the fridge.

"There's some apples," he says.

I take the hint. He doesn't want me eating junk. I grab an apple and start to head downstairs.

"What's your rush?" he says.

He wants to talk. "I got a practice tonight. And Shawna wants me to call her."

"Oh," he says and looks at me like I'm hiding something.

I *am* hiding something. Howcome he wants to talk when I'm hiding something? I'm hiding the fact that I had a shitty day, that I goofed up in Mr. Mooney's class and that I don't want to talk about it. These things happen and I get blamed for making them happen. What he doesn't know won't hurt him.

I get downstairs to my room and throw my coat on the floor. I can hear Mom. "Why don't you hang it up?" She's not even home and I can hear her. I do hang it up, on Saturdays, the day I'm supposed to clean my room. Who cares if I don't hang it up.

I float on my bed for a minute. Just lie there floating. I can hear the water gurgling underneath me. Water makes a funny sound.

It sounds so wet. I hear Dad creaking across the floor above me. Probably making something with eggplant in it. I hate eggplant more than I hate lentils. At least lentils are very organized. They are tidy. Lentils would hang up their coats. Eggplants are slobs, like me. They would lie on their water beds listening to the gurgles.

I should feel close to eggplants, but I don't. They are so uncivilized. When I'm an adult, I'm going to make my kids hang up their coats too. All my kids will be like lentils.

I admit it. I feel like an eggplant.

The phone is just out of my reach, on the floor. I know exactly where it is. It's under my coat, and I'm supposed to call Shawna. As I stretch for it, it starts ringing, scaring me half to death. My bed is gurgling, the phone is ringing, and my Dad is creaking through the floor.

"Hello," I say, "Lanny Eggplant here."

"What?" says Shawna.

"I thought *I* was supposed to call *you*," I say.

"Yeah, well, I was waiting," she says. "What were you doing?"

"I was just reaching for the phone," I say.

"Oh sure," she says.

"I was thinking about eggplants," I say, being honest. You might as well be honest with Shawna. She knows when you're bee essing. "And the phone was under my coat, so I had to move my coat to get at the phone and I was just doing that when you called me instead. Okay?" Really, this is no big deal. Why am I making such an issue about it?

"What's the matter?" she says.

"What's the *matter*? What's the matter with *me*? Nothing! You wanted me to call."

"Yeah, but something's the matter, I can tell." She always does this to me. And she's doing it again.

The last time she asked what's the matter, we got in trouble. No, *I* got in trouble. Let me explain. My parents don't like Shawna. They've never actually said they don't like her, but you kind of get the message when they ground you for two weeks and say she's not to come over here anymore. And it really wasn't her fault. It was mine. I invited her over after school one day, when Dad was out of town and Mom was at work. The thing is, I'm not supposed to have people over when neither of the parents are at home. Okay, so I'm running a risk. And I have to admit that my hormones were bouncing off the walls. Like, it wasn't as though I was just going to show her the weird plumbing in this place, although I did. (The pipe draining the kitchen sink runs the entire width of the basement about eyebrow high and will get you every time.) No, I had her in the basement here in my room to try out my water bed. She doesn't have one. And since she's on the bed, I might as well join her, right? I mean, it's my bed. And we joke around a bit, and kiss, and I even get to feel her breast, which is great because I've never felt one before and this is a first for me. But before things get too hot and heavy, we stop. Or I stop. And she says, "What's the matter?" and of all things I could be thinking about, I have to admit that I'm thinking of this tiny bald spot my Dad has on the top of his head. Why, I don't know, but I tell her. "Oh sure," she says. And right away I know she thinks I'm putting her down or something, and I try to kiss her to make her feel better, and I'm in the act of trying to kiss her when Mom walks in. Yeah. No amount of explaining in the world can fix that one up. But it does explain why my parents don't like her. They probably think she's after my virginity or something.

Anyway, this time I insist, "Nothing's the matter with me. Now why did you want me to call?"

"I know someone who wants to buy your piano," she says.

"I can't sell the piano, Shawna. I mean, it's not mine. I mean, it's *mine*, but it's not *mine*?"

"I thought you decided that it was yours and you wanted to sell it. I thought that's what we decided."

"We talked about it, we didn't decide about it."

"Are you serious?"

"Of course I'm serious. If I tried something like that, my folks would have my balls for bookends."

"Oh, great!"

This has an ominous ring to it. "What do you mean, 'oh, great'?"

"Well, why did you talk about it for?"

"Why did I talk about what? What do you mean, 'oh, great'?" I'm getting confused.

"I thought you were serious."

"I am serious. About what?"

"I thought you needed the money. I thought you wanted to sell the piano."

"Well, I do, but I can't."

"Oh, great."

"Would you stop saying that?!"

"Well, you don't know what the problem is."

"Then tell me, I didn't know there was a problem!"

"My stepmother is coming over to look at it!"

"Your stepmother is what?"

"She's coming ov—"

"Now?!" I interrupt. "Well, tell her she can't. It's not for sale!"

"She's on her way."

So this is the problem.

I go upstairs and look out the window. I don't know how much time I have. I try to act calm by whistling. What do I usually do when I'm calm? I do not whistle. I stop, quick. I don't want to give myself away. I've got to distract myself. Why don't I eat supper with Mom and Dad, like I normally do? Good idea, Lan. Sometimes I impress myself with my brilliance.

But it's one of Dad's meals. If we ever had real meat at our house, I mean like steak or something, my stomach wouldn't know what to do with it. It'd say, "Hey! What is this stuff? Are we supposed to digest this or what?" Dad is filling his face with eggplant. He really likes it.

"So how was your day?" Mom says to me. Mom is sort of picking away at the fake meat with some kind of tomato sauce on it. As much as I complain, it's not bad, really.

"Fine," I reflex. Then I add, "But kind of strange too." I decide to go for the sneak-attack knockout punch. "How would you feel about selling the piano?" I query, nonchalantly.

They both look at me like I have three heads.

"Why would you want to do that?" asks Mom.

"Well . . . " I might as well say it, "to raise a thousand dollars. You said if I raised a thousand dollars I could go to the Caribbean with you."

"No," says Dad, "we're not selling the piano so you can go to the Caribbean with us."

This sounds final.

"But it's mine, isn't it?"

"No, and even if it was, the answer would still be no."

It is final. It's hopelessly unchangeable, and to push the point any further would be an act of incredible stupidity. So, I continue.

"What if someone wants to buy it?"

"They would be out of luck, wouldn't they?" says Mom.

"Yeah, but what if they showed up at the door with a thousand dollars in their hands?"

"For one thing, they wouldn't have enough money, and for another, just what are you getting at here?" says Dad.

I pause. I might as well tell them.

"I think I sold it."

"What!" they say in duet. Dad just about chokes. In fact he does choke. Mom has to slap him on the back. He recovers with tears in his eyes.

"You *sold* the *piano*?" Dad wheezes, wiping his beard. Dad's beard can get a little bit messy from time to time.

"I didn't exactly sell it, someone is coming to look at it."

"Who?" says Mom.

"Shawna's stepmom." I'm not talking very loud. I can tell.

"Who?!" says Dad.

"Shawna's stepmother," I repeat a little louder.

"Shawna." Mom says her name like it explains everything.

"Who the hell said you could sell the piano!?" Dad is not enjoying this.

"No one," I say.

"Can you believe this?" Dad says to Mom. "I can't believe this."

I wish this was April Fool's, and I could just say, "April Fool's Day! Ha ha ha." But it isn't and I can't.

"Well, it was just a misunderstanding. We were kind of joking around, and I guess Shawna took me seriously. I didn't know her stepmother was looking for a piano." I think I'm making some headway here in explaining the situation, when I am doomed by the doorbell. Everyone looks out the window. A woman is standing at the front door. I've never met her, but it's got to be Shawna's stepmom. She has enough makeup on to stop a puck. "Good lord," says Dad. He looks me right in the eye and adds, "You handle it. You sold it, you can *un*sell it."

I get up from the table and go to the door. I open it and am immediately hit by the scent of the entire perfume counter at The Bay. It just about knocks me over. "Hi," she says, "are you Lanny Reich?" I nod. If I open my mouth, I'll gag. "I'm Shawna's Mom," she continues. "She says you have a piano for sale?" And she smiles at me with these big green teeth. Or is it her eyes?

I step back and tell the quickest lie I've ever told, "Ah . . . no, I'm afraid it's sold already," I say. I hear this sound in the kitchen. I'm not sure what it is. I think it's coughing.

"Oh, I'm sorry," she says, "I shouldn't be surprised. It seemed like such a bargain. Ah . . . I wonder, would you mind if I had a look at it? Just to make comparisons?"

"Ah, no, they picked it up already," I blurt. I can't believe me.

"Oh, that's too bad," she says.

Suddenly a voice behind me says, "Actually, Mrs. Ah . . . "

"Carpenter," says Shawna's stepmom.

"Mrs. Carpenter," says Dad, "we have a piano, but it's not for sale. I'm sorry you troubled yourself to come over."

"Oh," says Mrs. Carpenter. "Oh, well. Okay. Thank you." And she leaves.

Dad steps in front of me to close the door, me being too stunned to move. Why do I do these things to me? "Finish your supper," he says.

Back at the table, the three of us sit. No one is looking at anyone else. We might as well be eating cardboard. Nothing has any taste.

"Pass the salt," Dad says. "I don't understand. I don't understand. First you go try to sell the piano, and then, instead of just telling her the truth that it's not for sale, you say it's sold? I mean, what's going through your mind?"

"I don't know," I say. I really don't. It's a question I often ask myself, but not necessarily about me. I ask it about *them*.

"'I don't know' isn't good enough," says Mom.

"Well, I don't, but if I say it's not for sale, then I get Shawna in trouble."

"With her mother," says Dad.

"It's not her mother, it's her stepmother."

"Let's not split hairs," says my mother or whatever she is.

"Okay fine, I'm sorry. I goofed. I made a mistake. Can I be excused?"

"No."

I look up at the ceiling and around the room.

"Don't roll your eyes because we want to finish this discussion," says Mom.

We doesn't include *me*. I want to get out of here.

"If this is how you handle situations like this, I'd hate to see how you'd handle yourself if things really got tough."

Great. Now the lecture. My mouth feels like I've been eating hard-boiled eggs for a day or two. I reach for the milk.

"Don't go playing with the *milk now!*" says Mom.

"I'm thirsty."

"Then *don't spill it!*"

This is suddenly a very big deal. My manhood is resting on the line here. I spill one drop and I'm done. This is a test, a "testicle", and I know it. They're both watching me. I pour. Ve-r-ry carefully. I am trying to fake nonchalance. Faking nonchalance is different from just *being* nonchalant. Done!! I've done it! I didn't spill a drop! I'm trying desperately hard not to look smug. If I look smug, I blow the whole image.

One problem. I am concentrating so hard on not spilling anything that I've filled the glass too full. The only thing that's holding the milk inside the glass is surface tension. I know it's called surface tension because we took it in Mr. Mooney's class. I shared marks for knowing it. Now I've somehow got to get this glass to my mouth without spilling anything. I can't do it. I know I can't. All this faking nonchalance has taken too much out of me. There is another solution. I can put my mouth to the glass. This too will blow my image. But what the hell, I haven't spilled anything yet. I decide to go for it. I bend at the waist, and just as my lips touch the glass I look up at Dad.

My idiot father the poet is grinning from ear to ear. With eggplant on his teeth.

* * *

This is when I blow it. Literally. Milk all over the place. It is one of those tense situations when you're not supposed to laugh, and the harder you try not to, the more likely it is that you will. But what is he grinning at? You just don't know what's going on in their minds. Sometimes I think they know more than they let on. There's this whole theory that if aliens really did land here they couldn't talk to us if they wanted to because they know too much. It'd be like us trying to talk to ants or plants or something. I mean we're just too advanced for them. At least we think we are. On the other hand, maybe they think they're too advanced for us. At any rate, I have to clean it up.

It sort of puts an end to our open and honest discussion, which had a lousy beginning to start with and was going in an equally lousy direction. So it's only right that it has a lousy end. I've been grounded and the piano is still here. Which means I can't go out for a month, I have no money, and it's going to be a long, cold, lonely winter.

I'm sort of half-lying on my bed thinking about this, half-listening to the radio, and half-watching this ant crawl across the wall. It's the middle of winter. Where does this ant come from? He's all alone on this trek across my wall. Where's he going? Where'd he come from? I decide to follow the ant. He goes all the way up to the ceiling, then stops there. Puts his little antennae out and pokes around. Is he trying to get his signals straight or what? Then he turns around and starts heading back the way he came. "Don't be so stupid, you've already been there," I say. He doesn't listen. He keeps right on going. For some reason I am getting mad at this stupid ant. "Don't go that way, stupid, you've already been there." I'm actually saying this out loud and he suddenly stops like he heard me. The antennae start poking around again. He turns around and starts moving back up the wall, only in a slightly different direction. Where the hell is this stupid ant going? The situation between me and this ant is getting very strained.

The phone rings. I jump about a foot.

"Hello?"

"Hi Lan." It's Shawna. She's only said two words but I can tell she's PO'd. "Thanks, thanks a *lot*."

"For what?" As if I don't know.

"As if you don't know. For making me look like an idiot. My stepmom was really pleased. I mean, really pleased, you know?"

"Yeah, well, I'm sorry."

"And then I get the blame. It's all my fault."

"Hey, I said I was sorry, and some of it *was* your fault."

"It wasn't my idea to sell your stupid piano."

"It wasn't my idea either. It was Dozen's."

"So blame me and Dozen then!"

"Well if it hadn't been for you guys, none of this would've happened!"

"If it hadn't been for *you* none of this would have happened. It's your piano, you're the one who needs all this money, not me and Dozen! We were just trying to help!"

"Yeah, well, great help. If I want your help, I'll ask for it."

"You did!"

"Oh sure, and if I want help to kill myself, are you going to show me ways to tie a rope? Tell me what pills to get?"

"Don't be a jerk!"

"Maybe I am a jerk, maybe that's what I am."

"Grow up, Lanny!"

"*Me* grow up? *You* grow up!"

Well, you get the gist of the conversation and the direction it is heading. Off a cliff. It gets really personal and she says stuff about me not being able to handle my life or anybody else's. I end up saying stuff about her I shouldn't even repeat because it shows what kind of dork I can really be, but I called her a slut. Can you believe it? The perfect thing to call someone if you want to end a friendship.

I try phoning her back to apologize, but she hangs up.

I call Doze and explain the whole story and try to get him to apologize for me, but he says it's my problem and he's not going to touch it with a ten-foot pole. And this is a friend?

I've put on my Minglewood tape that nobody's ever heard of, and I'm lying on my bed, trying to blank my mind. Except I can't. I think about calling Boog or Maureen but I'm too depressed to move. And there, right above me, on the ceiling, is the ant. He's just booting it along, going to work, or going home to the wife and kids. I'm glad to see him. When you're feeling this low, you'll take any company you can get. He's probably the only friend I have. I assume that he's a guy ant. Then the thought occurs to me that maybe he's a she. It's hard to tell if you don't know. I don't know any of my friends too well.

Chapter eight

Things have been a little blah with me being grounded but it could be worse. They could have pulled the plug on hockey. It's about the only social life I have left. So I've been spending a lot of time hanging around the house. Not that I have a lot of choice.

Dad's by the microwave when the phone rings. He answers.

"It's Day-glo," says Dad with his hand over the phone. "You want to talk to her?"

"She's your sister," says Mom.

"I hate asking her favours. She always says yes to me. She's more honest with you."

Mom rolls her eyes.

"I'll let you talk to Colleen," he says. He goes to hand Mom the phone but the cord is too short. The phone clatters all over the floor. I feel for Aunt Daphy's ears.

"Oops," says Dad.

"For Godsakes," says Mom. She finally gets the phone to her ear. "Sorry, Daph. Sandy's doing his juggling act here . . . Yeah," she says, but "yeah" to what I don't know.

I like listening to half a phone conversation and filling in the other half with my answer.

It's a real ball. Of course, you've got to keep your mouth shut or you can get into real trouble too.

"So how are you doing? What have you been up to?" says Mom.

My answer, "You called to ask me that? I'm fine. I just got back from a trip to Zulon where I met Wayne Gretzky's lord and master."

"Oh, isn't that interesting," says Mom. (I bet I was close.) She covers the receiver and says to Dad, "She just got back from a trip." (See?)

"Listen, the reason I called is we wanted to ask a special favour of you and just wondered how you'd feel about it . . ."

My answer, "You didn't call me, I called you, but go ahead, shoot."

"Sandy and I are planning to take a vacation at Christmas and we were wondering what your plans were."

My answer, "Well, on Christmas I was going to Zulon, why? Do you want me to come?"

"No, actually between Boxing Day and January sixth. The problem is," and she looks at me, "is what to do with Lanny."

My answer, "He's no problem. Leave him with me."

"Do you think that would be possible? It'd solve everything for us. That would just be fantastic if you could, and Lanny would love it." She's nodding "yes" to Dad.

My answer, "Sure, he could make a whole bunch of ashtrays for you to fill."

"Oh sure, I'm sure he'd be happy too."

"Happy to what?" I say to Dad.

"I don't know," he says.

"Absolutely, it's the least he could do," says Mom.

"The least I could do what?" I ask again.

Dad shrugs with his eyebrows.

"Fine. I'll put him on." She hands me the phone.

"Hi, Aunt Daph," I say. "The least I can do what?"

"Hi, Lanny. Well, I've got a big craft fair coming up, and I thought maybe you could help me set up," she says.

"Oh sure!" Then it occurs to me. "Except I'm grounded."

"Not for that," says Mom.

"But Mom says it's okay," I tell her. "So when do you want to do it?"

"Next weekend," says Aunt Daph.

"Oh sure, no problem."

"Great. I wonder if you could come over Thursday and we can start getting ready," says Daph.

"Thursday? What time? I've got to practice piano Thursday." Piano practice gets in the way of anything I want to do.

"No, you don't," says Mom, "If she wants you to help, you can skip practice."

"Mom says I don't have a practice, so what time do you want me there?"

"Anytime after supper. Just come over and we'll start."

"Okay," I say.

"Well, this should be fun!" she says, "I'll see you then. Bye."

"Bye," I say and hang up.

It's all set. Two weeks with Aunt Daphy. It *should* be fun.

We say good-byes and see you's and for the moment everything has a little glow. A Day-glo I guess.

"I'm glad that's cleared out of the way," says Mom.

There is a little pause here. It's actually more of a vacuum and something is waiting to fill it. I pour myself a glass of water. I have given up milk. For some reason, I never spill water.

"Sandy," says Mom, watching me pour, "how is Daphne?"

"What do you mean?"

"Well, how is she? You know." Maybe someone knows, but I sure don't. Mom's trying to get at something here.

"Oh, she's fine," says Dad. "She's over that."

"Over what?" I say.

"Never mind," he says to me. Then to Mom, "That's long behind her. I mean, that was a long time ago."

"Yeah, well, you never know," says Mom, lighting up a cancer stick.

"Never know what?" I say. "You guys always do this to me."

"It's nothing you should concern yourself with," says Dad. "And neither should you," he says to Mom.

She shrugs her eyebrows. "Nice pour," she says to me. "So how's school?"

She's a master at changing the subject.

"Fine," I say. It's not really though. I mean school is fine, but the rest of my life sucks.

I can't stand it half the time. With Shawna and I not talking, it means the group has a serious glitch. I try to apologize to her, but she just ignores me. I haven't quite given up, but it's going to take time. And time is soon going to be interrupted by Christmas. Mall meetings are at a temporary standstill. Basically it's just Doze and I and Maureen at lunch and stuff, but Doze's going away at Christmas to visit his Mom in Vancouver, and Maureen is terminally hung up on Boog who is on the verge of getting kicked out of school. And Boog is on the verge of getting kicked out of school. He skips classes all the time and has started hanging around with some guys who I don't like much, sort of bikers, but none of them have bikes. One of them I know was busted for drugs. Another one is on probation for assault or something. I mean, he was always friends with them, and since our group broke up, he just started hanging out with them more. People can change so fast. One day everything is fine, the next it's all different. There was this girl in our school that a lot of people knew and liked and one day she just wasn't there anymore. She committed suicide. It's like, what happened? What goes on in people's lives that makes those things happen? And you want to do something, but you don't know what. It makes you feel empty and scared. What this all means is that I'm really looking forward to staying at Aunt Daphne's. It'll be a nice change.

Sure enough, Boog's not at school one day, and the word is out that the police caught him with a bunch of stolen stuff in his room. Boog, I mean Boog! I can't believe it.

At our next game, it was pretty quiet in the dressing room and not the usual horsing around. Everybody knows about Boog. He is in the corner getting his gear on and no one is looking at him. We are hardly looking at each other either. All it would take is one guy to ask what happened, and I'm sure the ice will break. So I screw up my courage and I say it.

"So what happened, Boog?"

You can cut the silence with a hockey stick.

"Nothing," he says. He doesn't even look up.

If it was quiet before, you can hear sweat drop now. Boog gets up and leaves for the ice. We all look at each other. We get up and follow. Nobody says anything about it or makes any kind of cracks. If you do, you don't know what's going to happen to you.

He is terrible in goal. We get creamed ten to three. But as bad as he is, it doesn't prepare me for what comes next.

CHAPTER NINE

The Moondog Fair is this big craft sale they hold every year at the Ex just before Christmas. As you can probably guess, all these people who make crafts get together under one big roof and try to cash in. The thing about most of these people is even though half of them are bald they still try to have long hair with what's left. Either that or they have beards, the men, that is. The women are missing the beards and they all have hair, except for one who is completely bald. They all dress the same, men and women. Rumpled. Sort of the colour of your back yard. And those that don't have long hair look like my parents, or kids from school who are trying to go back to the sixties. There's these weird old guys too, in plaid shirts and green pants who make these little wooden dancing puppets on a stick. There's little old ladies with blue hair selling lacy things, quilts that look like sky, pot holders that look like fish, and other stuff that grandmas make. There's clowns and jugglers and guys with guitars and violins (dead cats) filing through the aisles. There's artists with paints. There's artists with pencils, charcoal, crayons, mud, glass, sand, and leaves and some things I don't know what they are. There's artists with pens, brushes, knives, spray-guns and blow-torches, and just in case you forgot we're in the twentieth century, there's even an artist with a computer. There's jewelry and dingle-dangles and stuff made of wood, kites, dolls, enough stuff to make your head spin.

But more than anything, there are pots. Big pots, little pots, teapots, coffee pots, mugs, bowls, plates, vases, ashtrays, and things you wouldn't care to describe or couldn't if you would. There are more pots than you can shake a stick at. There are pots coming out of your ears.

And at least half of them are Aunt Daphy's.

I should know. I hauled them there, from where she lives, in her garage. Well, there is a house attached, but she essentially lives in the garage. Except she doesn't call it a garage, she calls it a studio.

If you've ever been to a potter's studio, you've got to agree about one thing — they're an incredible mess. There is more dried mud and dust per square centimetre than in your average desert. I mean a desert might have more sand but you know what I mean. This is especially true in the area by *the wheel*.

The wheel is a thing that spins mud into pots, assuming, of course, that you know what you're doing. You plunk a piece of mud, or clay

I guess, on the centre of this wheel, and you turn it. While it's turning, you cup your hands around the clay, and lo and behold! It becomes a cylinder. Then you take your thumbs and you push down into the middle of the cylinder while it's still turning, and it starts to get hollow, and before you know it, you've got a pot — or in my case, an ashtray, because I can't get the mud centred on the wheel in the first place. Anyway, the wheel sits in one corner of the studio.

Half the studio, which is about the size of a Camaro, is shelves. And on the shelves are row after row of pots and cups and all those things she makes. It looks like a little clay army stuck at attention, so neat and perfect. Brittle.

At the other end of the garage/studio is a miniature brick church that has pipes coming out along the floor. It's actually a kiln, the oven where she cooks her armies. And all around it are more shelves, where Aunt Daph keeps it after it's cooked. Her finished stuff is glazed in Coke and coffee-with-milk colours and has this shiny feel to it, like you want to touch it. That's the big stuff, all clay.

Then there's her little things, porcelain jewelry and dangles and little tiny sculptures. These are delicate and have delicate colours of blue and turquoise and the colours of sea shells. How one person can make all this stuff is beyond me. It's like going to some kind of strange beach where all the stones and pebbles on the shore are perfect and you want to take them home.

So I go over to her place on Thursday after school and she has about twenty wooden boxes of this stuff all packed like it was going to China, and we load it into her blue Datsun pick-up and take it to the fair which is only a couple miles away. That's the easy part.

The hard part is unloading it and setting it all up so it looks nice. I do the unloading, and Aunt Daph does the setting up. She has these light blue drapes she staples to the boxes and sets the stuff on that. It looks great, except that one wrong move and you're really afraid the whole thing's going to avalanche to the floor like a water-slide and you'll be standing there ankle-deep in ex-pottery. Especially with all these kids running around. I mean, we're not doing this alone. There's about five hundred other people there all setting up too. And they've all brought about ten kids each and said, "Go play over there," to get them out of their way. So there's these kids playing tag under your feet, and people yelling and tables scraping, and a half-dozen ghetto-blasters all tuned to different stations or playing different tapes, and people coming around to make sure you're certified, and to top it off, somebody's brought their dog. Either that, or he just wandered in through the open door and is looking for pats, or food, or a place to pee. All of which he finds. It's a nice dog actually, a gigantic orange lab with a big grin. But really, who needs it here? I've heard one crash already and hope we're not the next.

Then the lights go out.

Aunt Daphy is standing on top of the table and is in the process of placing this very beautiful large bowl on top of the display, when the lights go out. She screams. About five hundred other people plus ten kids each all scream too. The dog barks. I yell something like, "Don't move!" to Aunt Daphy. She yells back, "I *can't* move!" It's pitch black. And Aunt Daphy is standing on top of a table holding a large bowl.

To say there is a general commotion is, like, a severe understatement. I mean, I thought the noise was bad *before* the lights went out.

But somebody has found a flashlight and at least we now have something to focus on, something we can see. The general commotion dies down a bit, and the person with the flashlight shines it up onto their face, making them look like a Hallowe'en mask, and says, "Everybody just stay where you are! Don't move! The lights will be back on in a minute!" There are a bunch more shouts and yells and barks, and the flashlight wanders out of sight for a few seconds, and then the lights come back on.

Aunt Daph is in exactly the same position as she was in before the lights went out. Only now, her eyes have the same glazed look as one of her pots.

She sets the bowl down, turns, and, as though it was the greatest single truth of her life, she says, "My arms are going to fall off." And she lets them fall, and for a moment you actually think they're going to unhinge from her shoulders and drop to the floor. But they don't. They sort of flop to her sides and hang there, like the wings of a great big bird.

"I thought of jumping, but it's not high enough," she says.

It's moments like that you wonder what the heck she's talking about.

* * *

I didn't realize it on Thursday, but this has been a three-day commitment. I've spent every spare moment of my time behind this table sort of being a shopkeeper. To be perfectly honest about it, it's been boring. It's been incredibly boring. Aunt Daph knows it too. That's why she's gone to get me some junk food. It better be junk food. I'm tired of sprouts and bean spread. I'm dying for a Coke and fries. So I'm waiting here, Sunday afternoon, the last day of the fair, when Boog shows up. You can knock me over with a feather.

"Where you been?" asks Boog, like everything is hunky-dory.

I could ask the same of him, but I don't. "Right here," I say, "playing store."

"That's what your Mom said." Boog picks up a piece of porcelain jewelry. It looks like a leaf, only it has red and flecks of silver running through it. "This is nice."

"You break it, you pay for it."

"How much?"

"There's a price tag on it. What does it say?"

"Five bucks? For this?" For Boog, anything that costs more than sixty-five cents is right out of his league.

"It's hand-made," I say. "It wasn't just punched out by some machine in Taiwan."

"Yeah, but five bucks? I could get ten of these if it was punched out."

"Yeah, but it *wasn't*. That's the whole point, so don't drop it."

"Ooops!" he says, while he fakes dropping it. This annoys me more than it should for some reason, and Boog senses this. He gives me this don't-be-such-a-kid look, but he puts the leaf back. I can't tell if he wants to talk about something or if he's just hanging out being a general nuisance.

"So how's it going?" I ask, hoping he'll blurt out what a bunch of scum he's been hanging out with and that he's turning over a new leaf, I mean, besides the red porcelain one he had in his hand. Instead he says something that surprises me.

"We broke up."

"Who?" I have no idea what he's talking about.

"Me and Maureen."

"I didn't know you were going out." I really didn't. I mean he used to look at her like he wanted to, but I thought it ended there. "What happened?"

"I don't know. She gave me a note. She says she just wants to be friends."

"Oh yeah," I say, knowing what *that*'s all about. The words are always something like, "I really like you, but I just want to be friends." It means get lost. I think I had my first note in grade three. I had my last one in grade nine. I'll probably get a few more before I die too.

"What happened? Did you have a fight?"

"No. She just gave me the note."

I don't know why he is telling me this. These are the first words he's spoken to me in weeks. I want to talk to him about it some more, but a lady carrying a little baby starts poking around the display.

The baby has these wide-open eyes the size of pie plates. The mother's probably in her twenties, just over the hill. She picks up one of Aunt Daphy's little dangly things from right next to Boog's leaf, and she wants to look at it more closely.

But the baby grabs it and throws it on the floor.

Boy, is that kid fast!

We all sort of stand there stunned. The dangly thing is in a million pieces — the only thing that's left is the price tag.

"Oh, good lord!" she says.

The baby says nothing.

"How much is that? I really must pay for it."

"Boy, is he ever fast," I say.

"It's a she," she says.

Meanwhile, Boog picks up the price tag. "It's five," he says, showing it to her.

"No, no, it's all right," I say. "It wasn't your fault. I mean, you can't blame her either."

"Well, then I . . . How much is that bowl up there?"

"The bowl?"

"The one up there on the top."

"That . . . " I say, knowing that no one is going to pay fifty dollars for it, ". . . is fifty dollars."

"I'll take it," she says.

Who am I to argue? The lady pays for it, has me wrap it in about fourteen layers of paper and then put it into a bag. She disappears lugging the bag and the baby into the crowd.

"That's one way to make a sale," says Boog.

"Yeah, Dozen would like that," I say.

But Boog doesn't respond to that. Instead he says, "How come if I drop it, I've got to pay for it?"

"Because you know what you're doing."

"So, what difference does that make?"

But before we get a chance to turn this into an argument, Aunt Daph shows up. She's loaded with fries, a hot dog and a Coke. I love her. "Would you take this?" she says, her hands full. I do. Boog sees this as a chance to leave.

"Hey, well, I got to go now. See you later at the game tonight, Jaw. Bye."

"Yeah, see you." He wanders off, one hand in his pocket.

"Where'd the bowl go?" asks Aunt Daphy.

"I sold it."

"You sold it?"

"For fifty dollars, but I threw in one of those dangly things so they thought they got a deal."

"Oh, I see," says Aunt Daphy. "My red leaf."

"No, not the leaf. That other thing, that was next to it."

"Oh? Well the leaf is gone too."

"Is it?" I'm looking.

"I wonder where it went," wonders Aunt Daphy.

I bite into the hot dog. I know where it went. There's only one place for it. Boog's pocket.

Chapter ten

Normally nothing gets in the way of my game. Even if I have an off night, I'm usually at least *there*. But tonight, nothing. And what really annoys me is we're winning eight to three. Boog is so hot, he's stoning them cold. Dozen's having a good game too. He's got a hat trick. I don't even have an assist. You'd never guess I was on the ice.

It's after the game and Dozen has to leave right away because his Dad is right there ready to go. But Boog is sitting on his bag in front of the window still waiting for whoever is going to pick him up. He's got a Coke and is staring at his reflection, pretending as usual that he's looking through the window. He can see me coming.

"Nice game," he says.

"Yeah, for you maybe." I throw down my bag and sit. I hang on to my sticks though, butts down, blades high.

"No," he says, "I mean you, *you* had a good game."

A liar as well as a thief? "Are you kidding? I might as well have stayed at home."

"I thought you had a good game."

"I didn't touch the puck once. I had a minus three tonight."

"Oh yeah? They only *had* three goals."

"Exactly, and I was on for all three." This kind of kills the conversation for a minute. He knows what I want to talk about. And I know he knows. I just don't know how to bring it up. I twirl the blades above me.

"Snowing," I say. You can see big fluffy snowflakes by the street light in the parking lot.

"Yeah," he says.

Snow is not a very hot topic of conversation, not that snow can ever be hot. And there's really something else on my mind that I want to know about. "So what did you take that leaf for?"

"What?"

"That red leaf, from my aunt."

"What are you talking about?"

"Oh, come on, this afternoon, at the fair."

"I didn't *take* anything! What are you talking about?"

"You took a silver and red porcelain leaf from my aunt's display table this afternoon at the Moondog Fair!"

"You're full of crap!" he says.

We stare into each other's eyes. I don't know what he's thinking, but if he says he didn't, well then, maybe he didn't. I mean, I didn't actually *see* him do it. I just saw his hand in his pocket. I realize I am holding both sticks across my lap in my fists like I'm getting ready to cross-check him.

I look away. Out the window. Boog's mother has pulled up. She's waiting.

"Your ride." I look back at him, and his eyes are glued on me like gum. I'm glad he's not Maureen or I'd have holes in me by now.

He gets up, picks up his stuff, and heads for the door.

He gives me one last look and leaves.

I'm sitting there, still clutching my sticks, wondering what's happening. I see him get in the car, their old beat-up car, and drive off. Then I see me, in the window. I stand. I'm taller than I think. I pick up my bag and start for the door. How come nobody is what they seem to be? The door is stuck. I mean, you think you know somebody, and really you don't. I bang the door with my shoulder. *I* go through, but my *bag* gets jammed. This is ridiculous! I can't even go through doors anymore! I yank my bag through and stand outside in the cold night.

Those big fat flakes are still falling. One of them lands on my nose. I can feel it melting. I'd like to scratch it, but my hands are full. I start thinking about snowflakes, how every one is absolutely and totally different and that Eskimos have two hundred names for snow. I'm thinking all these wonderful thoughts about snow and Eskimos and things, trying to forget about Boog,

94 YULETIDE BLUES

and I'm not watching where I'm going. I'm actually gazing up at all these zillions of different snow flakes falling.

That's when I slip on a patch of ice and fall. Like an idiot, I somehow crack myself on the head with my hockey sticks and see stars for a few seconds. Then I think I am going blind, because my right eye is blurry, I can't focus, and then I taste salt on my tongue. I know what this is.

I'm not going blind, I'm just bleeding to death.

CHAPTER ELEVEN

Getting cracked on the head proves hockey is a violent sport. Whether you're playing it or not.

Of course I don't die, but I just about give Mom a heart attack. Dad's impressed too. He drives me to the hospital for stitches. I've never had stitches before. I feel a bit like Frankenstein, sewn up like a football. At school, everyone wants to know the gory details. Everyone but Boog.

At noon, Dozen and Maureen and I go to the mall. This is the last week before Christmas break. We haven't been here since the last time all five of us were together, so it's a little bit strange, only the three of us. And today we're supposedly shopping. Everything's decorated up in lights and tinsel with greens and reds and fake snow. It's like a TV commercial. It *is* a TV commercial. There's half a dozen Santa Clauses wandering around. If I was a kid, I'd be very confused.

And then there's the music. Each store is playing its own. If I hear another Christmas carol before I die, it'll be too soon. And that's too bad, because I *like* Christmas carols, I really do — every year, for about a half an hour.

But too much is too much. There's this guy who's always *dreaming* about a White Christmas. I wish he'd *wake up*. And I personally think that someone should get the Little Drummer Boy off the streets. I mean, what's this kid doing out playing drums in the middle of the night? Doesn't he have a home? He should have a social worker. My mother, for instants, could place him with a rock band. He'd be happy there.

Christmas really is my favourite time of year. But you have to be a millionaire to do all the buying and selling you're supposed to do. I've got thirteen dollars and fifty-two cents. That's what I've saved for Christmas shopping. I have a very short list. Mom and Dad.

We're wandering around looking at things. And people keep looking at me and the patch on my head. I feel like a celebrity with all these eyes on me. Even the mall cop wakes up from his permanent nap to raise an eyebrow. He's leaning against a wall, across from Boog's fountain where we stop. It's decidedly hot in here and just looking at the water cools you off. But Maureen wants to keep moving.

"Let's go," she says.

"Hey, look at that!" says Doze.

"What?" we say.

"The money's gone!"

Sure enough, all that money that was in the fountain is gone. Just a few rust stains at the bottom.

"I wonder where it went?" says Dozen, and suddenly runs across to where a mall cop is trying to keep his eyes open.

"I wonder how they got it out?" I have this image of some guy in rubber boots with a shovel.

"I don't know, I'm boiling," says Maureen and she starts to pull her SunIce up over her head. For a second her sweater rides up and you can see her midriff, but while her SunIce is still half over her head, she pulls down her sweater with one hand to keep from undressing herself in public.

"Need a hand?"

"I'll break your arm," she says, looking right through me.

Meanwhile, Dozen returns. "They gave it away to the Salvation Army for Christmas presents."

And that's when I notice the dangly thing hanging around Maureen's neck. It's a red porcelain leaf, with silver flecks running through it.

"Maureen, where'd you get that?" As if I didn't know.

"Hey, that's nice!" says Dozen. Neither of us are in Maureen's morning classes, so we couldn't have seen it before.

"Michael gave it to me."

98 YULETIDE BLUES

"Who?"

"Boog," she says. Nobody uses Boog's real name. Except Maureen, I guess. But I've never heard her use it before.

"I thought you guys had broken up?" says Dozen.

"We're still *friends*. He gave it to me this morning. He said it's for Christmas."

"If you're still friends, howcome he's not here?" asks Dozen.

"Because we're *friends*, we're not going out."

Dozen looks at me. He doesn't understand. She probably thinks that I don't understand either, and I don't. But that's not what's on my mind.

"Do you know where he got that, Maureen?" I know she doesn't know. I don't know why I'm asking.

"No, why?" she asks.

I look at Dozen. I'm not saying a word. I know something that nobody else knows, except me and Boog. Or should I say *Michael*. He's all of a sudden a different person — maybe I should call him by a different name.

"Howcome you're calling him Michael all of a sudden?"

"He asked me to. He said that's what I could give him for Christmas, to call him Michael." Maureen's eyes are doing their usual thing. They're looking right through me. But Dozen is the one who sees something. "Your aunt makes those things, doesn't she, Lan?"

I look at him. "Yeah." I can't tell if Dozen is one step ahead of me, or one step behind.

"He stole it, didn't he." He's one step ahead. I look away, into the fountain where all the money's gone. I'm not going to say anything.

"F-ff . . . !" says Maureen, just about doing something I never heard her do before. Swear. This is about as close as she comes.

She rips the leaf from around her neck. "Would you give this back to your aunt?" There's tears coming in her eyes. She puts the dangly red porcelain leaf into my hand and walks away in a very big hurry. Dozen follows her. I do not.

* * *

It's one thing when you find out something about your friends that you don't particularly want to know, but it's a different thing again when you find out something about yourself that you don't particularly want to know.

I am an unforgiving coward, a weasel. All I can think about is how to get back at Boog. I don't care why he did what he did. But he lied to me, he stole from my aunt and he made Maureen look like an idiot. He hurt us. I'm going to hurt him back. An eye for an eye.

This is what I do.

I know today we're going to have one of Mr. Mooney's little quizzicals, a test. I know how he sets up. I just have to get there early.

I'm standing in the hall just down from the chemistry class, Mr. Mooney's, and I make sure he can't see me. It's the first period in the afternoon. I see him go into the class to set up the overhead projector getting ready for the test. As soon as he leaves, I rush in, take the test and then leave. I hope no one sees me. Then I go to Boog's locker and slide the test sheet through the top of the door. The whole thing takes me about thirty seconds. The warning bell goes. Then, in a big hurry, I go straight to the staff room and knock on the door.

Miss Feldman, the drama teacher, answers. "Yes?" She doesn't know what a good actor I am, because if she did, she'd have me up on the stage with the drama club.

"Can I see Mr. Mooney, please?"

"Just a minute," she says, and I can hear her calling, "Jack, there's someone here to see you."

Jack comes to the door, hiding a cigarette behind his back. I didn't know he had a first name. "Hi, Lan, what can I do for you? What happened to your head?"

I pretend that I am breathless and just got in from outside. I *am* breathless, but not for the reason I pretend. "I got hit by a hockey stick,"

I say, then I limp a bit to show him I can hardly move, "and I twisted my ankle too, but it's okay. Are we having a test today?"

"Of course, we always have a test Tuesdays, you know that. Why?"

"Oh, because I was talking to Boog and he said we weren't and I wondered if I could be excused to go see the nurse, because my ankle is, like, sore."

"I don't know where he got that idea — we're having a little test — but you can certainly go and see the nurse if that thing's bothering you."

"Oh no! It's not that bad. I can go after class. I can't afford to miss another one. I mean, I didn't do so good last week."

"Actually you did very well. You picked up the class average by a couple of marks."

The bell rings.

"Yeah well today I got to pick up *my* average by a couple of marks." And I hobble off, like my ankle is broken. It takes me forever to get to class, even though it's ten metres away. Mr. Mooney beats me.

I'm just getting to my desk when he's ready to start the test. He's turned the light on the projector and is about to remove the piece of cardboard, but he hesitates a second and says, "You should really go see the nurse, Lan. You can write this another time."

"No, I'm okay," I say. But I'm obviously in great pain.

"You sure?" he says. This is actually quite touching. No one has ever seen Mr. Mooney show such concern.

"Yeah, sure, I'm fine."

"Well, in spite of the fact that it was rumoured there was not going to be a quiz today . . . " He lifts the cardboard.

White light shines off the screen.

The class cheers. They think Mooney's giving us a Christmas present. I cheer too.

But the cheering stops like somebody chopped it with an ax. Mr. Mooney's look is the ax. "Where is it?"

You can hear a pin drop.

"Where is the quiz sheet?"

Nobody moves.

"Either that sheet shows up, or nobody leaves here till it does. I don't care if we're here till Christmas." He's so mad, he's practically whispering this. And it's so quiet, we don't have any trouble hearing. All eyes are on Mr. Mooney, Jack. All eyes but mine.

Very slowly, I look at Boog.

Interestingly enough, so does Mr. Mooney, Jack.

"Mr. McLellan," he says to Boog, "do you know where it is?"

"No."

Jack looks at me. I look down. He looks back at Boog. I look up.

"Can I see you a minute, Mr. McLellan?" And he leaves the room. Everyone watches in silent amazement as Boog half-stumbles to the door trying to look calm and cool. As soon as he's gone, a rush of whispers pick up like a wind in here, blowing through leaves. But there are no leaves, except for the one in my pocket.

I can feel two very small holes burning in the back of my head. I turn because I know Maureen is looking at me. Her face is totally expressionless. She is just looking at me. I turn away. *She knows*.

A couple of minutes pass. Speculation is high on what's happening. Suddenly Boog walks through the door. He's followed by Mr. Mooney. Mr. Mooney has the quiz sheet and the class resumes as if it's normal, only it's not. There is a tension in it you can feel, with mitts on.

We all share Boog's mark. I get a ninety-two and I'm very careful to limp out of class when it's over. I go see the nurse. She suggests I get X-rays, because she can't find anything wrong. If it still hurts tomorrow, I say I'll go. She thinks that's a fine idea. I limp out of the office *on the wrong foot*.

What a lie. I should be shot.

CHAPTER TWELVE

Today is the shortest day of the year, literally. It's about fifteen minutes long. The sun isn't up till after nine. And it'll be dark by four. You might as well just go in a hole and hibernate. Then come out in spring when the grass is green, and the birds are singing, and the leaves are back on the trees where they belong.

But I'm glad school is out. That last week was ugly. At least we get a break from that for a while. Nobody's normal anymore. What is it about Christmas? It seems to bring out the worst in people. Mom and Dad are snarling over Christmas trees. Every year they do this.

"Why kill a perfectly happy tree to set it up in your living room?" says Mom, and I've got to admit, she has a point.

"It's a *symbol*," says Dad, "of life." Weak, Dad, very weak.

"Oh, so you want a *dead* tree in your living room to *symbolize life!*" And again, I've got to agree with her.

"You want a *plastic* tree?" says Dad. This is always the kicker. Mom does not want a plastic tree. So they declare a cease-fire, just like in real wars at Christmas. They always declare a cease-fire, not because they want peace, but because they want a break. We end up with a real tree in the living room.

* * *

Not only is everyone getting ready for Christmas, but for the great vacation as well. Five days to departure. You'd think they were going to the moon. Maybe they are.

Mom has bought herself a new bathing suit. She even showed it to me, on. Personally I think there should be more to it in the way of cloth. The top comes down kind of low. I mean, for a mother, because she jogs and everything, she's got legs that come all the way up to her waist. There's not enough cloth there either. And she's as white as a snowbank, of which there's plenty outside.

"Mom, aren't you embarrassed?"

"About what?"

"About showing all that skin."

"No." She says. Very cool.

I mean really, normally she wears sweaters that come up to her earlobes and skirts that scrape the floor. I never knew she had so much skin.

"Guys are going to whistle at you, Mom."

"No, they won't. Your father will be with me." She's got a point there.

YULETIDE BLUES

"They'll probably laugh then."

"They can whistle or laugh whatever they like," she says.

"You'll burn," I say.

"No I won't. I got this." And she pulls these plastic bottles of sun-tan lotion out of a drugstore bag. There's about five of them, with different numbers on them. "Sunscreens," she says.

"You wouldn't need them if you had more cloth on your bathing suit," I say.

All she does is laugh. Very funny.

Dad's bought a new bathing suit too. He's got the opposite problem. His doesn't show enough skin. Where he found it I don't know, but it looks like one of those things you see in old photographs. The trunks come down to his knees with a matching top — that's got sleeves. If you throw in a scarf, he could be dressed for a football game in Regina, in October.

"Very flashy, Dad," I say.

"Don't you like it?"

"I think you should trade with Mom."

* * *

I go shopping at the Mall. This time I have to buy something. I get Mom one of those "Week-at-a-Glance" books. She likes those and uses them a lot. I also get her some of those packages of bubble-bath things. She likes to soak in the tub from time to time and read. She might as well smell nice while she's doing it. But Dad, what am I going to get him? He's impossible to buy for. It's not that he has everything, but what do you get a poet? Paper? I should get him a roll of hockey tape. When I was little, the first time I ever went Christmas shopping with Mom, I wanted to buy Dad a roll of black hockey tape so he could tape my hockey stick. It seemed like such a good idea at the time and Mom wouldn't let me. I can't remember what I eventually got him. I am actually standing in front of the paper and pens section when Maureen walks up. She's loaded down with bags.

"Hi," she says. Outside of class, we haven't seen too much of each other since the last time we were here.

"Hi," I say. It's good to see her. It really is.

"You got your stitches out."

"Yeah, my Dad took them out." It was like major surgery. "So what are you doing? I mean, I can see you're *shopping*."

"I'm supposed to meet my Mom."

Since she's got about fifteen minutes, we decide there's enough time for a Coke, in fact, *lots* of time because Maureen's mother is always late.

"So where's Dozen?" she asks.

"He's in Vancouver, you know that."

"Oh, right. To visit his Mom. Shawna's visiting one of her Dads." I must look at her funny because she adds, "Oh sorry, I forgot."

"Don't be," I say, "I've tried calling her. I don't have anything against her. I mean, I don't know what you heard but it's really all my fault."

"You should tell *her*."

"I try, I try."

"Don't try, do it," says Maureen, sounding vaguely like my mother.

The place is crowded. It's like those beaches you see on Channel Two that are jammed with birds. One wrong move and you get pecked in the head. We sort of sit there a minute sucking on straws, waiting to get pecked. And then it just turns into one of those ugly pauses. I don't know what to say to Maureen. We don't seem to be able to talk about the things we have in common, like Shawna, Boog or Dozen, because if you talk about one of them, you automatically are talking about the other. I try to think of something else, but my mind just spins wheels. I try to think what she might be thinking. I can't.

Then Maureen gives me one of her patented looks. Right through me. "Howcome you set that thing up in Mr. Mooney's class?"

"What?" This catches me off-guard.

"You know, stealing the quiz and making it look like it was Boog."

"What makes you think I did?"

"Well, you did, didn't you?"

I guess there's not much point in denying it, "Yeah," I say.

"So howcome you did it?"

"I don't know, to get back at him, I guess. For taking that thing from my aunt."

"You shouldn't have."

"Why not? He doesn't know."

"Yes, he does."

I get a funny feeling, way down deep. I think it's fear. "How?" I ask. "How would he know?"

"The same way I do. He just knows. I knew right away. He'll get you back, you know."

This makes me feel very uncomfortable. It makes me feel alone. It's funny how alone you can feel sometimes. I mean, here we are in the middle of a mall, trying not to get pecked by all the wildlife around us, and we're both all alone. Alone together. It's a strange kind of sad feeling. She looks away.

"My Dad said I can't go out with him anymore."

"Are you? Going out with him?"

"No. Not because of my Dad though. I just don't trust him."

"What do you think he'll do?" I jump back a couple steps in the conversation, because that's where I'm really at.

"To me or to you?"

"He wouldn't do anything to *you*, would he?"

"No, probably not. He's already done it to me."

"What?"

"Hurt me. He'll hurt you too, except it'll probably be physical."

Oh, great, something to look forward to, death and maiming. I think I'm depressed.

"This is depressing, you know that?"

"Don't be depressed. It's Christmas!" She suddenly bounces, all bright and cheerful.

"How can you do that? We have this depressing conversation about how we're both going to die and all of a sudden, whoopdidoo, it's Christmas."

"Well, it is."

"That makes it more depressing. On top of that, I don't even know what to get my Dad."

"Your Dad?"

"Yeah!"

"I bought mine a spatula," she says and pulls out this thing the size of a fly swatter. "He always makes hamburgers outside on the barbecue and burns himself."

"That's a good idea," I say. "Now he can do it from the living room, and he can swat flies at the same time."

This strikes Maureen as pretty funny and she laughs, swatting imaginary flies in the living room. I notice the people next to her make a little more room. In fact, even *I* make a little more room.

"What's so funny?"

"My *dad* can never find the fly swatter." She can barely get this out, she's laughing so hard. I guess it's even funnier than I think, because, lo and behold, I start laughing. Then suddenly she stops.

"What does your Dad do?"

"You don't know?" I thought everybody knew.

"No, how should I know?"

"He's a poet." Here we go again.

"A *poet*?"

"Yeah, he writes poetry."

"That's neat," says Maureen, "I know what you should get him."

"What?"

"A pencil sharpener!"

"A pencil sharpener?"

"One of those little ones that run on batteries. Yeah."

Right then Maureen's mother arrives, all loaded down with bags and boxes. A serious shopper. Maureen gets ready to leave, and just before she does, she turns to me and says, "Talk to Shawna." Then she smiles and says, "Merry Christmas."

I would like to talk to her, I really would. I don't know how.

I buy my Dad a pencil sharpener. A little one, that runs on batteries. I'll put it under the tree and hope he likes it. No, I know he'll like it. Even if he doesn't, he'll say that he does because that'll be his way of saying he loves me.

The reasons I'm going to tell this part of the story, the family Christmas part, is because I figure you don't know somebody unless you know the family. I mean I can go on and on about all kinds of stuff, but you won't really know what it means unless you understand the family and the way it works. The thing about Christmas is that it's the time of year when the family gets together.

The other reason is that as near as I can figure out, there's two ways to experience Christmas: as a kid and as an adult. This is probably the year I'm half-way between, so I will get to see it from two points of view.

The final reason is this is the good part, before the bad part.

Chapter Thirteen

It's not always easy to believe in such things as "Christmas Spirit", but, when everything comes together, and with a little help from your friends, why not? I mean, go for it. What I think it is, is this: waiting for the fat man to come down the chimney. You buy all your gifts, you get everything all decorated up and ready, then you wait.

It's the waiting that does it.

And it's not just like waiting for your marks, or waiting for the bus, or waiting after school, it's waiting for something you know is going to be *good*. It might not be exactly what you had in mind, but whatever it is, it's always good. The whole day.

At our place, we always do the same thing. It's like a ritual and it starts on Christmas Eve with eating. The rest of the year, everybody's always harping at you, "Haven't you had enough?" and, "You're going to get fat," but at Christmas, anything goes. You can fill your face till the cows come home, and believe me, the cows are nowhere in sight. Dad makes these chewy things that are all right. They have figs and oatmeal and healthy stuff in them, and to be polite you always have a couple, just to please him, but it's Mom who gets into the spirit of Christmas. Mom makes these Nanaimo bars that are obscene, I mean, they should be banned they are so decadent. They make the ones at the Moondog Fair taste like dogfood — and they weren't bad. I don't know, she puts something in them, almond bits or something that lift them right off this planet, and you just can't leave them alone. We usually have about a plate of those *before* we go over to Grandma's place.

It's at Grandma's place where the eating really starts.

Grandma and Grandpa Reich are Dad's parents, if you didn't already figure it out. And because they're German, they have all this German food which they try and stuff you with immediately. Grandma isn't happy unless she sees you with food in your mouth. Which explains why Grandpa is sort of fat. I mean, the old guy is trying to keep the old girl happy. Consequently, he has high blood pressure and knees that he can't walk on half the time. That's why he's going to the hospital for an operation. I'm sure if he just cut down on Grandma's cooking he'd be fine. On the other hand, Grandma'd think he didn't love her or something. So what do you do? It's kind of sad, but I think she's going to kill him. It's the price you pay for being happy.

Between Mom's Nanaimo bars and Grandma's decorated shortbread cookies, mincemeat tarts, raisin butter tarts, home-made turtles (which are especially totally excellent) cherry pies with ice cream, as well as assorted nuts, rock candies and chocolates, there's nothing to complain about — except for maybe a slight pain in your stomach.

Anyway, this is where we go on Christmas Eve, and Mom and Dad bring their gifts to Grandma and Grandpa, and Grandma and Grandpa give their gifts to Mom and Dad and me and we all sit around and eat. Then after we've been there for a while, and we've admired the tree and the little nativity scene with baby Jesus and Mary and Joseph and the shepherds and sheep made of plaster underneath it, and which has been there ever since I can remember, and we've eaten Grandma's goodies till we're stuffed, Grandpa brings out his home-made wine.

This is part of the ritual.

You can see Mom and Dad sort of bracing themselves because they don't like home-made wine much, especially Grandpa's, but they drink it anyway because he's so proud of it. And there's usually Christmas carols playing in the background because Grandma has this Mario Lanza record she plays at Christmas that she's so proud of. So along with the eating and drinking home-made wine, there is a lot of talking, half of which is boring, and half of which is in German which I don't understand. And neither does anybody else. I mean, Dad knows a bit, but not enough to carry a conversation and sometimes Grandma and Grandpa start babbling away in German, forgetting that the rest of us don't know what's going on. But when they're talking about me or Aunt Daphy, *then* I listen because you never know when you're going to pick up a tidbit you might find useful sometime.

Like Mom says, "Lanny's head is healing nicely," and Grandma will come over and feel all over my head like she was a surgeon and say, "Yes, it is. Just like Sandy's head, he too so nicely healed." (She talks backwards like that.) And she launches into this description of Dad when he was a baby pulling a radio down on top of himself. I guess radios were bigger then and weighed a tonne because they were made of wood. And she paints this picture of my Dad as a little baby crawling on the floor looking for stuff to do when he gets the idea that playing with a radio would be fun, so he pulls it off a table, down onto his head.

And Grandma and Grandpa both continue with stories of how Dad nearly killed himself doing this and that till he was practically an adult, while Dad sort of sits there with this silly grin on his face hearing his life story told in front of him. I can't believe he was such a klutz. I would have disowned him by the time he was three.

Sooner or later, but always before midnight, everyone wishes everyone else a Merry Christmas and we go home. This is so Mom can phone her parents, who live in Kelowna. Every two or three years we go *there* for Christmas and the ritual is pretty much the same — except for opening the presents. In Mom's family you get to open one present before midnight. There's only one rule that governs this, and that is it can't be something big. Mom is in charge of this, because it's sort of Mom's way of being "home". So Mom hands out three presents, all from her parents, the McNeils. There's one for me, one for Dad and one that she actually hands to herself. "Here Colleen, one for you," and she holds a present up in the air with her right hand and then grabs it with her left. It's sort of cute if you know my Mom.

One thing about her parents, they sure know how to wrap things. It's like a major struggle to get the wrapping off. You practically have to be a burglar to break into these things, and not just me, but Mom and Dad too. There's a reason for this: in our house you're not supposed to tear the wrapping paper. It's not like we save it or anything, but if you tear it, it's like cheating. Don't ask me why, that's just part of the ritual.

Dad is the first to get into his and he laughs. It's a little tiny brush and comb set, for his beard. There's a tube of wax with it too, for his moustache, which he plasters on right away, then combs one end up and the other end down. In the meantime, Mom and I have opened ours. I get one of those neat pairs of folding sunglasses that race car drivers wear when they're just toodling around in their Porsches, and Mom gets a book called *How to Make Money Doing Social Work*. She laughs too. I guess it's supposed to be funny.

Then she calls home.

Mom talks first, then Dad and I, all saying Merry Christmas and thank you and some other stuff about the weather and that sort of thing, then Mom talks again and says good-bye. After that we do only one more thing before we go to bed. It's a little bit corny but we actually do it.

We sing "Silent Night".

Mom always starts, and you never know what note she's going to start on, but it doesn't matter because she always sings soft, and Dad and I join in for "Holy Night", usually singing two different notes besides the one that Mom is singing and it probably sounds like wounded cats trying to drag themselves off the street. But we sing it anyway, actually together, even though it's hard to look one another in the eye, because it really is a little bit embarrassing. It's like wanting to say, "I love you," but being afraid somehow. Still in all, by the time we're near the end of it, we're all singing full force and we couldn't give a care what we sound like. We do love each other. It's Christmas.

* * *

When we're done, we go to bed. Actually, *we* don't go to bed, because *somebody* stays up and fills the stockings. And to be perfectly honest, I don't know who. You'd think after fifteen years I'd figure it out. I've never heard anybody doing it, and in our house that's something, considering how the floors creak every time you move. You might think that I'm a pretty sound sleeper, but I think the real reason I haven't figured out who fills the stockings is because I don't want to. And there they are, hanging by the chimney with care, stuffed in the morning with stocking stuffers, candy and an orange always in the toe. This is what we open first, *before* breakfast.

It seems that I'm always up first. It's seven o'clock. I've been lying in bed since six-thirty. I wait till seven just to be civilized. In some ways I can't believe I still do this, but hey, I'm improving. In the old days I used to get up at five. Christmas just isn't Christmas without the ritual.

I get up, throw on my bathrobe, and go upstairs. I grab all the stockings, go into my parents' room and say, "Merry Christmas!" Then I hand my groggy parents their stockings and sit on the bed and we all open them together. This is like the warm-up band before the real concert. It's fun and gets you in the mood. I get some socks and an old Beatles button (why?) you pin to your shirt plus a package of razor blades, ha ha, real funny. I started shaving a while ago. But I also get a real nice shaving brush that's sort of like Dad's which of course he never uses. And I wonder for a minute what he looks like without his beard. Among other things, Dad gets these little ducks that he thinks are pretty funny. They're little ones, a mother and a whole herd of little ducklings. I guess he wrote some poems about them once and so it's kind of a joke from Mom. Mom gets a little book on how to quit smoking, which strikes her as pretty funny too. She also gets some perfume that she really likes. I like it too. It's called "Wish". Dad calls it "Swish". He says she can drink it when she gets tired of wearing it.

This is all before the main event, opening the stuff under the tree. Before we do that, we have to get dressed and have breakfast. *We*, all of us. I can do this in about five minutes flat. However, the parents take hours. They don't seem to have any idea that time is passing here, that it'll be New Year's any minute now if they don't hurry up. I can't imagine what takes them so long.

Finally, we sit down for breakfast. It's seven-thirty. Yesterday Dad was making these things he wouldn't let anyone see. That's what we're having for breakfast. And they are incredible. They are cinnamon rolls with pecans and sticky syrupy stuff on the bottom. These might just be the best things he's ever made. It beats all heck out of lentil stew. I demolish two of them in five minutes and I've tried to eat them slow. It's seven-thirty-five.

Now Mom has to have coffee and a cancer stick. This is taking forever. She stinks the place up while I wash the dishes to kill time. Dad plays with his mustache wax. He puts it on his eyebrows to make them stick out like sun visors. Neat, Dad. Between the two of us, we manage to kill another five minutes.

I don't believe it! Mom goes to the bathroom.

"Come on, Mom!"

"Nature calls," she says.

"Can't you go after?"

"I am going after. I'm going now too."

Mom can be so insensitive, I mean, for a saint.

Dad parks himself under the tree. "We're waiting!" he says.

"We're going to start without you!" I say.

"Don't you dare. I'll be right there," says Mom and the toilet flushes in a pretty big hurry.

Finally, finally, finally, we're all there. Dad hands me the first gift. It's from Grandma Reich. It's probably a sweater. She always gives me sweaters. And I can't complain, she has great taste. I really like it. Except that this is a very heavy sweater. As I unwrap it, I can see that it is a sweater, but there's something in the middle of it, a board? Yes, it's a board, a dartboard! What am I going to do with a dartboard? I don't even have any darts.

Along with the sweater and dartboard, I get lots of things, the most neat of which is a very stupid-looking penguin from Mom. It's wearing a tux and stands almost to my knee. What makes it neat is this very quizzical look it has on its face. I decide to call him Jack, after Mr. Mooney our chemistry teacher.

Mom thanks me for the date book, but what's she's really tickled about is this pulse counter Dad got her. It looks like an oversize watch with a wire leading to a little case around her finger that has some kind of sensor in it to keep track of her pulse rate when she's jogging.

She wants to go and try it out right now. But it's twenty below. She's going to wait till it's warmer out. I don't blame her. She also gets a little envelope that contains the rules to about fifty different kinds of dart games. There seems to be a pattern emerging here.

Dad has sharpened every pencil in the house. My pencil sharpener is a big hit with him. I don't have the heart to tell him it wasn't my idea, that it was Maureen's. I guess it doesn't really matter, as long as he's enjoying it. Mom also got him this green-and-white scarf that's about twenty feet long. He's got it draped around his neck looking for more pencils to sharpen. It doesn't take a whole lot to make Dad happy. Because he's also got the darts.

I've got the board, Mom's got the rules, and Dad's got the darts. I think we're supposed to co-operate.

There's always that lull after opening the presents. And in that lull you always wish there was more — not that you're greedy or anything, it's just that you're sad that it's over, that you've been waiting for this and now it's done. Besides, what do you do now?

Well, for starters, you clean up the wrapping. Then after that, you can either hang up the new dartboard and figure out the rules of that, or a word game my Dad got called

YULETIDE BLUES

"No Kidding". Since we've got all those sharp pencils, we opt for the word game.

It's one of those bluffing games, where you get a word and you make up a meaning for it. And the person who gets the most votes for their made-up words wins. Of course Dad loves this game. He knows he's going to be good at it. But guess what? Mom turns out to be very good at it too. It's neck and neck with them to the finish. And she wins. Dad is almost heartbroken. It's like he's playing defense and somebody slipped around him and put the puck in the net. If he had a hockey stick, he'd slam it against the boards. Instead, he challenges her to a dart game.

First, we've got to find a place to hang the board. This is not going to be easy, because as I said before, our basement has a low ceiling with a pipe running through the middle of it and there's really no obvious place to hang a dartboard. I offer my room, but it's turned down because they don't want to put holes in my wall. So we finally settle on this space on the wall at the bottom of the stairs. The only problem with it is that if you're coming down the stairs in a hurry and you don't know there's a dart game going on, you could wind up with a dart in your ear. So while Dad is measuring the correct height for the board and getting hammers and nails together, Mom is working on a sign. The sign says, "Danger! Dart Game in Progress." And she draws a little head with a dart sticking out of it.

The game we decide to play is called "Around the Clock". You have to get a dart in all the numbers on the board — in sequence, beginning with one and ending with twenty. But before you even start shooting at the numbers, you have to throw a dart in either the outer ring, the inner ring or in the bull's-eye.

I don't know if I'm going to be very good at this game because it's taking me quite a while to even get close to the bull's-eye. However, I'm better than Dad. He doesn't even hit the board with his first three darts. And then on his second turn, he sticks his second dart in the ceiling. Mom just about pees herself laughing. She says she'll have to put the warning sign outside. I'm not sure Dad is real amused. I think he thinks what I've been thinking — Mom's been practicing somewhere. She's hit the inner ring and is already going for two.

This is turning into a grudge match. I mean, it is a grudge match already with Mom winning the "No Kidding" game, but let me put it this way, if this was a hockey game, the sticks would be getting high.

Mom hits three.

"You've been practicing," says Dad.

"Sandy, I've played about three times in my life."

"Well, howcome you're so good at it then?"

"I don't know, I'm not! It's just that you're so terrible." And then she giggles. This is like throwing gas on a fire. Dad throws another dart. It glances off the board and sticks into the bottom step. Mom laughs. Dad glares.

"Okay, I won't laugh," says Mom. And she tries to hold her face in neutral. This is not going to be easy because Dad throws another one into the ceiling.

Mom laughs. Dad glares.

"Honest, I won't laugh again."

"It's not that funny," says Dad.

"I know, I know, it's just that . . ." and she breaks down into a fit of giggles. It's contagious. I giggle too. Dad looks like he's thinking of throwing darts at *us*. He'd probably miss. I giggle even more.

"What are you laughing at? You're not doing so hot either," he says to me.

"I know." I'm still smirking.

"Do you guys want to play, or do you just want to stand around laughing at me?"

This straightens us up.

Dad hits the bull's-eye.

"It's hard to concentrate with people laughing at you," he says.

It's Mom's turn. This time *she* throws it at the ceiling. This strikes her as even funnier than when Dad does it. But she collects herself and at least hits the board in her next two shots.

My turn. I come close, but no cigar.

We settle into a steady rhythm. Dad starts hitting some. Soon, we're all within two or three of each other. Mom's still leading. But she's been on seventeen for a long time. I get lucky and hit a couple of doubles and pass her — shooting for eighteen.

Dad hits a triple and is suddenly tied with Mom.

The game is getting grim.

"We should take this with us this afternoon," says Dad. We're going back to Grandma and Grandpa Reich's this afternoon, except that we won't be alone. All the available relatives will be there too — for Christmas dinner. The thought of this makes Mom miss the board. But before Dad can feel too good about the miss, Mom says, "Yes, we can play in teams, me and Mike against you and Vera." This is hitting below the belt, because Aunt Vera and Dad do not get along. I don't know why. But whatever it is, you can cut the tension between them with a knife.

Dad gets lucky. He actually bounces one off the ceiling and is now tied with me, at eighteen.

YULETIDE BLUES

Uncle Mike is Dad's little brother, although you'd never guess it by looking at him — he's about three feet taller. Dad calls him this German word, *Schaskopf*. It's about the only German word I know. Anyway, Uncle Mike and Aunt Vera have two little kids who can cause more damage in the blink of an eye than any ten ordinary kids — the screaming midgets, Sean and Tara. They're three and four.

Mom hits eighteen. We're all tied. Now would be a good time to quit. I suggest this and just about get cuffed in the ear.

"And deny your mother the pleasure of losing?"

"You're tempting the fates," says Mom.

"Fates, shmates," says Dad, and ricochets another dart into the step. Poor Dad.

I hit nineteen.

Mom and Dad both miss.

I hit twenty.

Mom and Dad both miss.

I triple out.

Dad hits the ceiling. "Where the hell did you learn to play like that?!"

"Just beginner's luck, Dad," I say.

"Bull! You've been practicing."

"I have not. Where am I going to practice?"

"I don't know where you've been practicing. But if you put half the effort into your piano . . ."

"I have not been practicing!"

"How could he be practicing, Sandy? He just got the game this morning," says Mom.

"You too!" Dad says, or, "You two!" I don't know which, but I walk up to the dartboard and take it off the wall.

"What are you doing?" he asks.

"What does it look like?"

"Hang that back up!"

"No."

"Lanny, stop behaving like a child."

"Who's behaving like a child?" This is not a cool question to ask your father, even if he is a poet.

There is a very nasty moment of confrontation here that if it was on the ice in a hockey game would actually lead to violence. I got the dartboard ready as a shield.

But he looks at me and says, "Me."

Knock me for a loop or what.

Then he turns and climbs the stairs. Mom gives me a look of disgust and follows Dad upstairs.

Howcome I feel like the villain? Just what went on here? Standing there with a dartboard in my hands, I vow never to say or do anything again. I will just *be*. What a stupid way to end Christmas morning.

Chapter fourteen

I always forget what a sore loser Dad is. Maybe it's because he was never good at sports. I'm just assuming he was never good at sports, because I've never seen him play any. Mom says he used to be a pretty good swimmer, that he used to compete in a club and go to swim meets and stuff, but I've never heard him talk about it and the only time you ever see him in a bathing suit is on the beach, where he sits reading books while he's turning red from sunburn. He never tans. He goes from white directly to red. Then he peels and goes right back to white again, no pausing for brown in between.

It's funny how life just plows ahead. I'm still trying to figure out what happened this morning while we're on our way to Grandma and Grandpa's, and Dad is still in a lousy mood. If he was a little kid, he'd probably go into the garden and eat worms. Then we'd be sorry. When he's in a mood like this, I wish he'd stay home and write poetry. When he's writing poetry, he gets this glazy-eyed look, like a fish that's been hit on the head. He spaces right out — from another planet. But now, he's looking for worms to eat. He's no fun to be around.

It should be interesting when he tangles with Aunt Vera. We know it's going to happen because it always does. And you know what I'm going to do? Exactly nothing.

The first thing we do is ooh and ah at the presents. Dad sort of grunts. Grandma gets this huge tackle box the size of a boxcar. She can carry a boat in it. Maybe it *is* a boat. But she loves it. And Grandpa's got one of these little things for putting golf balls. You putt at it, and no matter how far you miss the "hole" by, the machine returns the golf ball to you. It's great, even I like it. Dad of course steps on a golf ball and hurts the sole of his foot. Something else for him to grumble about.

For some reason I've brought Jack, my penguin. I introduce him around and he handles himself well. He even gazes quizzically at old Aunt Florence who greets him cordially. She leans out of her wheelchair and pats Jack on the head. Tara, my little cousin, isn't too sure about him. They're about the same height, and she doesn't trust him. He's too still. Sean, on the other hand, wants to tackle him and boot him all over the house. He's just a bit bigger than Jack. Uncle Mike laughs. He says Jack looks like Dad and Aunt Vera agrees with him. This pleases Dad no end. He's lost at "No Kidding", and darts, he's hurt his foot, and now he looks like a penguin named Jack. If he wasn't so growly, it'd be funny. It's funny anyway. Jack laughs. Or is it me? It can't be me. I vowed not to say or do anything. One of us laughs.

For two kids only about the size of Jack, Tara and Sean can sure make a lot of noise. It fact, it amazes me how much noise they can make. And how they can be in so many places at the same time. Sean wants to push Aunt Florence in her wheelchair. He thinks it's a baby-carriage or something, and every time he tries, he gets a shot from either Aunt Vera or Uncle Mike. It doesn't stop him from trying though. He just yells louder. Poor Aunt Flo doesn't know what to make of the whole thing. She wants to say, "Just let him be," but she knows the little guy could put her through the picture window, head first in a snowdrift. So she sits there and smiles. A fixed smile. A broken smile?

What is it about that smile?

"Vut are you tinking?" Aunt Flo is talking to me in her funny English.

"What?"

"I see you looking at me."

I must be staring at her. "Oh, sorry. I was just thinking of something."

"Oh. Iss . . . "

She probably wants to keep talking but I'm gone, I'm history. I see little Tara about to nose-dive into the couch. I make like I'm going to rescue her from certain doom. I'm really just rescuing myself. What a jerk. Staring at your aunt. But, what is it about that smile? Sort of like the Mona Lisa. Dad likes her though, and not just because she gives cheap piano lessons. He calls her the Grand Old Dame. G.O.D., that's what it spells.

So G.O.D. sits there with her Mona Lisa smile and I'm surrounded by screaming midgets, and we're all waiting for Aunt Daph to turn up. If she doesn't show soon, Dad is going to take a bite out of Aunt Vera's head. I don't say this for any reason other than I'm getting hungry and Dad has muttered something about Aunt Vera being a turkey. The smell of a turkey cooking also happens to be filling the air, and it's coming out of the oven any second now, crammed full of stuffing with steaming potatoes, carrots, those jellied salads, and gravy. Drool. Come on, Aunt Daph, what's keeping you?

Grandpa has decided to fill the time by filling glasses full of his home-made wine. He even gives me some, watered down with Seven-Up. I ask for a glass for Jack too, but everyone thinks this is a pretty good joke and he doesn't get any. I notice Dad drinks his in about one gulp and is reloading already. So is Uncle Mike.

Aunt Vera and Mom and Grandma are in the kitchen trying to burn the house down, which is to say, not only are they cooking, but they're also smoking. It's kind of funny, they all smoke the same brand of cancer sticks, so aunt Vera puts her name on her pack just so it won't be confused. I never really noticed it before, but only the women smoke. The men eat. If Grandpa smoked, he'd be six feet under by now. Dad said Grandpa smoked two packs a day till he was forty. Dad also said that when he was in university, he used to smoke too. He didn't say what.

Grandpa's wine must have suddenly become very tasty because Dad and Uncle Mike don't seem to be getting enough. I personally think that they should be feeding it to the screaming midgets. Maybe it'd slow them down a bit. And maybe a drop or two to Aunt Florence, to wipe that grin off her face. It's got to the point where I can't look at her anymore. Not that I could look at her much in the first place, but now, forget it. You sort of wonder what goes through the mind of a person like that. You never know.

But whatever it is, it's not cars.

That's what Dad and Grandpa and Uncle Mike are talking about, cars. Uncle Mike is some kind of expert on cars. He buys old ones then fixes them up and sells them. So whatever he says, goes — at least when it comes to cars. But Dad, for some reason, is trying to tell him that Japanese cars are better than American cars.

"When you consider the engineering . . . "

"What do you know about engineering?" interrupts Uncle Mike.

"You don't have to be an engineer to recognize good engineering, *Schaskopf.*"

"Oh, I see. So you can just walk up to any car and tell me if it's engineered right."

"Yeah."

"Yeah, you're full of it." Uncle Mike knows how to end a discussion. And turn it into an argument. "You think you bloody well know everything don't you."

"Mike, that's enough," says Grandpa.

"Listen, you little shit, I know more in my little finger that you do in your whole *being!*" says Dad.

"Boys!" says Grandpa. But they're not boys, they're men. *I'm* a boy.

"Right! If you know so much, why don't you get a job?!"

"What?"

"Get a job instead of bumming off your wife."

This has brought everybody to the living room. Nobody wants to see a fight, but it's like a car accident, everybody watches anyway. The only thing is, I thought it was going to be between Dad and Aunt Vera, not Dad and his brother. But not a soul is stirring, not even the midgets. All that's moving is the pulse on Dad's forehead, and the smoke from three cancer sticks.

"You want to go outside?" says Dad. This is not really a question, it's a challenge.

Uncle Mike walks to the door, puts his hand on the doorknob and says, "After you." He opens the door.

"He writes!" I say, and can't believe I say anything after vowing not to. I have also managed to grab the centre of attention, and now that I have it, I don't know what to do with it. So I say more: "He doesn't bum. He writes." Uncle Mike is looking at me like who the hell are you and where did you come from?

Everyone is standing around with their mouths hanging open. "Yeah," I add, like *he's* the bum and the rest of us are saints. I have just made things ten times worse and I don't have a dartboard to hide behind. Which is too bad because after Uncle Mike's done with Dad, I'm next. What we need now is a miracle.

And a miracle happens.

Billowing in through the open door walks Aunt Daphy, loaded down like Santa Claus.

"Thank you, Michael, Merry Christmas!" she says and plants a big kiss on his cheek. "Merry Christmas, Sandy!" and she kisses Dad. Then she notices that no one has moved. She looks at Dad, then at Uncle Mike. Then back at Dad again. "Were you two going out?" she asks.

Uncle Mike is still standing there attached to the doorknob. "Ah, no," he says and closes the door.

"Good. I've got presents for everyone!" And she starts unloading herself, and the midgets start screaming, and Aunt Florence starts smiling, and things go back to some semblance of normalcy. "They're not big presents, but they're very special!" says Aunt Daphy. She doesn't know it, but she's already brought everyone a present. It's called PEACE.

CHAPTER FIFTEEN

Aunt Daphne has this effect on people, like there are *Things of a Higher Order* you should get concerned about. Before you can say Wayne Gretzky three times, Uncle Mike and Dad are shamefacedly shaking hands. I can't explain it. Maybe there are *Things of a Higher Order*. You know Aunt Daph thinks that way by the kind of gifts she gives.

You never know what you're going to get from Aunt Daphy. Last year she gave everybody tickets to a lecture by some guy from somewhere else in the solar system, I mean *really* from another planet. Dad and I went to see him. His name was Mada, if you can believe that, which is of course "Adam" spelled backwards. He said that he was "an off-planet being" and his job was to get everybody ready for the harmony convergings or something like that. It had to do with the planets all lining up for some reason or other. And then he said things like, "I am me and you are truth," and he kept on talking about the "lights within", which at the time reminded me of those Rolaid commercials where the guy's stomach lights up and glows.

Dad had this funny look on his face the whole time, this quizzical look, like Jack.

Anyway, half her parcels are things like herbal candies and mint tea bags, but she also has this little case of paints. She calls the midgets to her.

"Okay, Tara? Or Sean? Who wants to have their face painted first?" This is what they're getting for Christmas.

"We'll be having supper soon," says Vera, with this what-do-you-mean-paint-my-kids look on her face. And of course as soon as the midgets hear that it's not cool to have their faces painted right now, just guess what they both want?

"Okay, Sean," says Aunt Daphy, "we'll do Tara first. She's smaller."

And for the next ten minutes, you've never heard two quieter kids. They're like statues. First one, then the other. And while one is getting painted, the other sits and watches. She paints this kind of angel face on Sean, and it has the funniest effect, I mean, *odd* funny: Sean behaves like an angel. He calms down, is gentle, and stops trying to push Aunt Flo out the window. The same with Tara. She gets a clown face, and suddenly everything she does is funny, really funny, and she knows it. She has become a clown.

140 YULETIDE BLUES

While Aunt Daphy is painting the kids' faces, the rest of us are wondering if that's what we're getting too. Mom and Grandma and Aunt Vera are setting the table and getting the food ready to serve. Dad and Grandpa and Uncle Mike have opened another bottle of wine and have this look like they're ready to break out into song. Either song or war, it's hard to tell which. Me and Jack are collecting chairs from the basement and other parts of the house so everyone has a place to sit. But all this is just trying to hide what we're really thinking, which is, what are we getting from Aunt Daphy? Aunt Florence is definitely the odd man out. She knows what she's getting because Aunt Daph gave it to her already. She's wearing it around her neck. It's the red porcelain leaf.

* * *

"Oh wow!" says Aunt Daphy, "Too much, this is *wonder*ful!" She's talking about the spread in front of us. It's all there: turkey, stuffing, gravy, cranberry sauce, potatoes, carrots, the works.

"Too much I don't know," says Grandma, "but it should be enough." And everyone digs in. The food gets passed around once, in a neat and orderly fashion, then after that, you're on your own. Everyone has a glass of Grandpa's murky wine in front of them, mine is cut with Seven-Up, so that we can toast the season. The only ones who don't have wine are Tara the Clown, Sean the Angel, and Aunt Daph, who has painted a wreath on one cheek and a bell on the other. They have milk.

Grandpa does the toast. He lifts up his glass and says, "Here's to a wary merry," and he looks at Uncle Mike and Dad, "unt *peaceful* Christmas." And everyone clinks glasses with everyone else, even the midgets.

You've got to like Sean the Angel, he spills his milk. But what do you expect? The kid's only four. I help him clean it up. I'm very good at it. Tara is getting bored, but instead of yelling about it, she builds a snowman on her plate, out of potatoes. She gives him a little carrot hat. It's cute. Then she eats it. "I eat a hat," she says.

After everyone has eaten enough for about a week and a half and is so stuffed it hurts, Grandma brings out the desserts. You have a choice here: ice cream and mince pie or pudding with hard sauce. It's funny that no matter how full you are, you can always make room for dessert. I have the pudding with hard sauce. Dad has both. So does Uncle Mike. The rest of us aren't such pigs but secretly wish we were.

Now we really are full. I mean I could not stuff another crumb into my mouth. My body is saying to my brain, "Why are you doing this to me?" and I don't have a decent answer. I can't move. What if I had to play hockey right now? I'd die. I'd croak. Thank God I've got till Wednesday.

Mom and Aunt Vera start cleaning off the table, and Grandma asks if anybody would like coffee now, and most people accept. But Aunt Daph has a different idea. "If anybody would like tea, I'll read your tea leaves," says Aunt Daphy. Then adds, "I have lovely mint tea."

So this is her Christmas present. I see everyone is jumping up and down with joy.

"I'll have tea," I say.

"Me too," says Mom.

"I'd love tea," says Aunt Florence.

"Can I have tea?" asks Sean.

"Sure, you can have tea," says Aunt Daphy, "and I'll read your tea leaves too."

"Can I have pee?" says Tara.

"Vera, I think Tara has to go to the bathroom," says Uncle Mike.

Someone is confused here. I'm not sure who. But they haul Tara away to the bathroom, while Aunt Daph starts making the tea.

This is it. The big tea-leaf reading by Aunt Daph. Me and Mom and Aunt Flo, and Sean thrown in for good measure. But first we have to drink the tea and leave some leaves on the bottom. I knew she did this kind of thing, but it's the first time I've ever been a part of it. For some reason, I'm a little bit nervous. I don't know how serious I should take this. If I'm as serious as Aunt Daph, that means I believe that Mada is "an off-planet being" — which I don't.

When I drink tea, which isn't often, I take it with lots of milk and sugar. Except that you aren't allowed to have milk in this tea because then you can't see the leaves at the bottom of the cup. So I just take lots of sugar. Sean dilutes his with Seven-Up. He adds sugar too. "Mmm-good," he says, "it tastes like a candy cane." It does too.

"We'll do yours first," Aunt Daph says to Sean because he's pretty well gulped his down. She looks in his cup. "Where're your leaves?"

"In my mouth," says Sean making a face indicating he doesn't like them much.

"Well, spit them out, back into the cup," says Aunt Daphy.

Sean's quite happy to do this, but what it leaves in the cup bottom doesn't exactly help digest a big meal. It turns your stomach.

However, it doesn't seem to bother Aunt Daph at all. "I've never seen anything like it before. This is *wonder*ful!" she says.

Yeah? Gross me out.

"You, Sean, are going to grow up to be a big man, just like your Daddy. And then you're going to get a new pair of skates."

"I did already."

"But!" This is phoney. Give me a break. "You're going to get a new baby sister!"

I tell you what. Very suddenly, you can hear a *hair* drop. I mean, everything's frozen. Aunt Vera looks at Uncle Mike. Mom looks at Dad. Grandma looks at Grandpa. And Aunt Florence smiles.

"When?" says Sean.

Aunt Daphy looks Aunt Vera right in the eye and says, "You'll have to ask your mother."

"How did you know?" asks Aunt Vera. She is crossed between being very stunned and very mad.

"The leaves," says Aunt Daph. "Who's next?"

"When?" says Sean to Aunt Vera.

"Just never you mind."

And just as suddenly, everything goes back to normal, as though nothing had happened — even though something sure did happen and we're not sure what.

"I'll go next," says Mom and hands Aunt Daph her cup.

I'm going to drink mine real slow. I want to be last, way last, like next year sometime.

"Oh this is interesting," says Aunt Daph. "You're going on a trip."

"You know that, Daph."

"No. I know you're *planning* a trip. This says you're actually going."

"Oh."

"And, you're going to have to make some tough decisions — a tough decision, just one. And someone you know is going to have a personal tragedy." She looks at Mom and smiles. "That's it."

"A tough decision and a personal tragedy, eh?"

"Not yours, somebody else's," Aunt Daphy says brightly. "You next?"

"No, I'm not finished yet," I say.

"Well, Flo, I guess it's your turn."

This should be a real ball. Aunt Flo's future. She hands Aunt Daphy her cup and waits while she looks at the leaves.

Aunt Flo has stopped smiling, or at least isn't smiling the same way she was earlier. I've never noticed before, but she has sad eyes, and her skin looks thin, you can almost see through it. Her hands are very large, almost like Aunt Daphy's, but Aunt Flo's fingers are thin. They are elegant. She moves them in slow motion. Even when she plays piano, they seem to move like that, in spite of the fact they're actually moving fast. Sort of like giraffes running. It always looks like they're running in slow motion, but they're going at full tilt.

There is a general hush that's fallen around the room, and a sense of something weird going on here that started with Sean, continued with Mom and is increasing with Aunt Florence, the Grand Old Dame. I'm starting to wonder about Mada, the "off-planet being".

"Hmm . . ." says Aunt Daph, "there's fire in your life." Then she looks at Aunt Florence as though to see if she can take bad news. "And pain. Someone will hurt you. But you will live a very long life."

"Oh, goot," she says, "a wary painful, long life."

And everyone laughs.

"Oh no, no, the pain won't last long. It'll just be very intense."

This is reassuring. Something for Aunt Flo to look forward to — intense pain, as if she didn't have enough, living with a hip she broke two months ago when she slipped on some ice.

And now it's my turn.

"Oh dear," says Aunt Daphy, looking into my cup, "you're going to break something."

I think, "Hockey stick."

"And you will overcome a great fear, and make a new friend." She hands me my cup back, and smiles.

"That's it?"

"That's it."

This is a real let-down.

"Isn't that kind of general, Aunt Daph... I mean, 'make a new friend'..."

"If I was any more specific, you wouldn't let it happen."

"Yeah, but I break hockey sticks every other game. If that's what 'break something' means."

"It doesn't mean that."

"What does it mean?"

"I don't know, but it doesn't mean hockey stick." She finishes off her tea.

I feel like I've been Mada'd. Jack feels the same, or he *looks* like I *feel*.

"Why don't you do one for yourself? Read your own leaves?"

"I already have. I do one every day. And it keeps saying the same thing. 'I'm going to fall.' From what? I don't know."

I notice Dad gives Mom a little glance here. Like maybe he has an idea.

It turns out that the tea-cup readings are not the Christmas presents. The Christmas presents from Aunt Daph are truly unique. She gives everybody stones. Not just ordinary stones. These are special stones. What makes them special is this: they were given strength from the sun during the harmony convergings. This is not me talking, this is Aunt Daphy.

"The gem elixir was made from water that sprang from deep within New England, and because New England was once a part of

Atlantis it makes this water, this elixir, very special. (Of course, I knew that.) So these gems (I thought they were stones) and the Atlantis gem elixir were put into a special bowl that I made during the summer solstice and laid to rest for three days in the sun during the harmonic convergence. (I thought it was harmony convergings.) And the gems drew the power from the sun and the elixir, and that's what gives them their strength, and that's what gives them their power."

I told you they weren't ordinary stones. And they are in fact very pretty. There's amethysts for Grandma and Grandpa, rose and blue quartz, which Mom and Dad get, onyx, which I get, and obsidians for Uncle Mike and Aunt Vera. Sean and Tara get these big shiny crystals. They all supposedly come from Atlantis, or I guess you should say New England. Except for the onyx, which is pure black and comes from Mexico. The obsidian comes from a volcano. I don't know which one, but as far as I know there are no volcanoes in New England. You can use the stones for just about anything. I mean, you wouldn't want to go skipping them across the river, that'd be a waste of their strength and power. They're used more for things like curing and charming. I'm not sure what kind of things you can charm, but apparently you can cure things like warts and hangnails, and if you've got a really good one, you can cure cancer.

So anyway, that's what we all get. Except for Aunt Florence who gets the red porcelain leaf. But the story behind that is interesting too, because the red glaze Aunt Daph used to colour it, and the silver flecks that run through it, are all from some very special stones, from this guy Mada, the "off-planet being".

"It's a travel charm," she says, which strikes me as kind of funny, I mean where the heck is Aunt Flo going to go in a wheelchair? And then she adds, "For the journey of life."

You just never know about Aunt Daphy. Where she comes up with these things is truly amazing. And still it's fun. She always has this look in her eye like maybe this all a great big joke.

* * *

It was an interesting day. Christmas always is. And if you write off the time between playing darts and Aunt Daph showing up, it was a good day. After dinner we all played "Risk". Dad won. Finally, he won something. The only downer happened when Tara ate her stone. Well, when she tried to. Uncle Mike dangled her upside-down and squeezed her till it fell out. Aunt Daph was pretty upset. Other than that, everything was normal.

I suppose I'm not really acting my age, but what the heck, I take Jack to bed with me. I haven't taken a stuffed animal to bed with me for years, in fact, I can't remember the last time I did. He sort of has an interesting smell, like the inside of a new car.

And just as I'm cuddling up to Jack, there's a knock on my door. "Can I come in?" It's Dad. I don't know why he asks, because before I answer, he's already in. I quickly stash Jack sort of half under me. "Did I startle you?"

"Yeah," I say.

He sits on the side of my bed and puts his hand on my shoulder. "I just want to thank you."

"For what?" I ask.

He pauses and says, "For being who you are, I guess." Then he just sort of sits there for a year or two and looks at me.

"Is that it?" I mean who else am I going to be?

"Yes," he says, "that's it." And he gets up and kisses me on the forehead, something he hasn't done since, well, since the last time I took a stuffed animal to bed. "Good night," he says and leaves.

I know this is supposed to be comforting and things, but it isn't. Like it may be comforting to *him*, but not to me.

I lie awake for a time and stare at my blank wall. These strange images flash through my mind and it's sort of like watching a rock video on my wall, you know, when you watch them without the sound and they don't make sense. Half the time they don't make sense *with* the sound. But anyway, they're flashing up there on the wall, things about stones, and Atlantis and Dozen and Sean with the Angel face, Tara the Clown, Aunt Florence's hands — all sorts of things, they just keep on coming. It must be all the food I ate, because I think of food and eating, then all of a sudden I see the old buffalo in the middle of a field. He's eating Christmas cake. Then he looks at me, and he turns and runs away. And then it's like I'm the buffalo, and I'm running somewhere halfway home with people chasing me. And my legs get heavy, and I fall through space, and just before I land, I wake up. Which is hard to do, considering I didn't think I was sleeping. There's a lump under me. It's Jack. I pull him out from under me and I hold him. I'm tired and a little scared. I think of Aunt Daphne, and eventually I fall asleep. A jumbled grey sleep.

Chapter sixteen

It's Boxing Day. I wake up with fuzz in my mouth. I've been chewing on Jack in my restless sleep and feel like I've been emptied, like Tara was yesterday, grabbed by the heels and shaken upside-down. I'm anxious. Mom and Dad leave tomorrow. I also hear them creaking around upstairs. Everyone will be packing today, including me. I don't feel like it. I'll have all day. Did I ever have a lousy sleep. I ate too much yesterday. That's the price I pay. And it's late, eleven o'clock. I want to *do* something. Maybe I'll go play shinny this afternoon.

I wander upstairs and Dad is on the phone. "Daph," he mouths to me and smiles.

"Are you ready for your boarder?"

My answer: "With bells on."

"For Lanny, tomorrow!" A little alarm goes off. How could she forget? She's just joking, right?

He laughs. She was just joking.

"Yeah, well, the reason I'm calling is we didn't talk about money. We should help out with groceries. He eats like a horse."

I do not.

"And milk. He spills as much as he drinks." He looks at me. I look at him with what I hope is a disgusted look. "But he's getting much better about that." Thanks, Dad. I mean, I never spill a drop other places, just at home.

"I know, but we will anyway. And he'll have four games, we've got the dates here . . ."

"I can tell her," I say. And she's probably said the same thing.

"Okay, but you can get him there, eh? He can get himself to the practices." I always do.

"Right. Fine. Bye." Dad hangs up. But you can tell something is on his mind.

"What's wrong?" Mom asks.

"I don't know. She didn't sound right." I hate it when things don't sound right. It always means something is wrong. But hey, if anything's wrong, it's too late now.

It's afternoon and only about ten below with a bit of wind. Mom has gone jogging to test out her new pulse counter, and I think it's time for me to head for the rink. There's two of them near here. One's indoors, that you have to rent, and the other is outdoors, and it's run by the community association and is free. That's the one where all the shinny happens when it's not too cold out. Once you get moving around you hardly even notice that you're outside.

There's already about thirty guys there, most of whom I know from school, and a couple of girls, one of whom is Maureen. I'm surprised to see her, although I shouldn't be because she's apparently a very good ringette player and she must have to practice once in a while. I've never seen her play. I should go sometime. Anyway, there is a couple of games going on, one with skates, with five or six guys and Maureen, and one without skates — real shinny — with the rest of the guys. They are played across the width of the ice, which is very full of snow and needs a scraping real bad.

I'm glad I brought my skates, even though I wasn't planning on using them if there was a good game of shinny going on. But because Maureen's here I think it'll be kind of fun to play with her — or against her — depending on how it works out, for a while at least. I can play boot-shinny later.

Maureen is pretty good, and just to show off, she uses the butt end of her stick to move the sponge puck around. She doesn't do this all the time, just now and then for laughs. What surprises me is how quick she is. Don't misunderstand me, she's not fast, she doesn't have speed — I can outskate her — but she has quickness. And she's aggressive. I also notice that she's sweating, something you don't expect to see every day out on the ice — I mean from a girl. There's even a little bit of checking, nothing hard enough to knock you off your feet, but enough to let the other person know you're there. The other guys aren't backing away either. It's good fun and we've been at it for about twenty minutes, when who should show up but Boog.

Boog doesn't have his skates, because all he owns are goalie skates and he hates playing goal in shinny anyway. Instead he has this old toothpick he must have had since grade four that he likes to wheedle around with. But that's not the interesting thing. The interesting thing is how he acts towards us. He's all smiles and friendly to us and acts like we're long-lost buddies, which I suppose we are, and convinces us to take off our skates so we can go play shinny together.

So this we do.

Shinny is a lot of fun. It doesn't matter how many people are on each team, in fact the more the merrier. That's because you're not on skates and you can't cover as much ice in the same amount of time. And since no one is on skates, the ice isn't making as much snow and the surface is much more slippery. So it's important to wear shoes that have some grip. But somebody's always falling and there's a lot of laughing.

It turns out that Maureen and I are on one side, and Boog is on the other. I notice that Maureen isn't as aggressive playing boot-shinny as she was on skates. I wonder if it's because

Boog is here, or because she feels outnumbered by all the guys. There is one other girl, but she's on the other team.

It's amazing that people don't get hurt because no one wears equipment and it's really quite crowded. But it somehow makes the competition more fair or even, and it's not often that you see someone play dirty. And just as I'm thinking this I get the puck and try and make a few moves towards their net, when all of a sudden, I'm hit. Very hard.

I'm lying on the ice and I can't get my breath. All the air keeps going out of me and I can't get any in. I'm making this funny little moaning sound, and I can't breathe. I'm afraid. I'm afraid I'm going to black out.

I get one little tiny breath in. But then I'm breathing out again, moaning. Everybody's standing around me. I can't breathe in. I'm going to die. What a stupid way to die. I get another tiny little breath in. I try to relax my stomach because that's what's happened, I've been hit in the solar plexus and that's why I can't breathe. But I'm still breathing out moaning. I can't believe I've got this much air in me. But I need more. I need it now.

This time I get a little more breath in, and I know I'm not going to die, yet. If I wanted to, I'd be able to focus on the faces of people around me. I know they're there, but I keep my eyes closed. I don't want to see who hit me. Somebody is holding my head. I open my eyes. I can't see who it is. It's still very hard to breathe.

"What happened?" I hear a voice say.

"He got hit," says someone stupid.

Somebody is lifting my legs.

"Don't lift his legs!" someone says.

"Why not?"

"You're not supposed to."

My legs get dropped. I moan. But I can take longer breaths now. And there is a pause here while people are trying to figure out what to do and nobody has any ideas. I have my eyes open, but I'm not looking up. I'm blinking, looking down at my toes.

"Are you all right?" It's Maureen. She's holding my head off the ice.

"Yeah, I'll be okay." I sort of check to see if all systems are go, and then I slowly get up. People help. They finally know what to do.

I look around.

Boog is gone.

"He got me back," I say to Maureen.

"I warned you," she says.

"I hate warnings," I say.

And I do, like that phone call this morning, when Aunt Daph didn't "sound right".

I suppose I should tell you I rounded out the day by walking Maureen home and her telling me Shawna was getting back from visiting a Dad later this week, not because it sounds particularly ominous, but in fact the opposite, it sounds good.

When things sound ominous, you never know what's going to happen next. When they sound good, you do. But I go to bed with this on my mind and my water bed gurgles ominously too. It's the bubbles that cause it to gurgle. I got to get rid of them, and while I'm at it, I'll add that stuff that keeps things from growing in the water. I think of things that might be growing under me, little microbes and stuff, in my water bed. I wonder what their life is like. I go to sleep. Ominously.

CHAPTER SEVENTEEN

It's the morning of the big day. They leave at five tonight. Dad's got all the passports and tickets and stuff all ready. He's debating whether or not he should take his pencil sharpener along. Mom's debating whether or not she should take her old bathing suit, "just in case". I want to ask, "Just in case what, Mom?" but I'm too busy debating whether or not I should take my ghetto to Aunt Daph's. It hasn't been working right. Only one speaker comes on. The whole place is a regular madhouse. And wouldn't you know it, that's when the phone rings. I answer.

"Hi, it's your quarter."

"I beg your pardon?" somebody says.

"Dad! It's for you." Nobody I know says "I beg your pardon."

Dad takes the phone, "Yes? . . . Yes, this is Mr. Reich." It's nobody Dad knows either or they wouldn't call him "Mr. Reich." Mom picks up on this too.

"What is it?" she says.

We watch Dad's eyes take on this kind of glazed look. It's like he's seeing something coming, something very large, and he can't get out of the way in time.

"What is it?" Mom says again.

"Yes . . . Yes, thank you," says Dad and hangs up. Whatever it was that ran over him did it with a paint brush. He is now a kind of off-white. There is a silence right now. It is a large silence, the size of those things that ran over Dad. He fills it with four words.

"Daphne's in the hospital."

"What happened?" asks Mom.

"I guess she attempted suicide again," says Dad.

* * *

Again, attempted suicide again. Now I know what all those looks between Mom and Dad were about. It gives you the chills, it makes you feel so helpless when somebody does that. Like that girl in school, one day she doesn't show up at school. Ph-fft, she's gone, dead. It makes you feel terrible. It makes you feel like maybe you should have got to know them better or something, maybe you could have stopped it. But here's Aunt Daph. I think I know her really well. I guess not. And even if I did, how would I stop it?

Anyway, we go to the hospital where she is. We're going to meet Grandma and Grandpa there. I've never liked hospitals. Let me put it another way. I *hate* hospitals.

Aunt Daph is on the fifth floor. If you know anything about the hospitals around here, the fifth floor is always the psych ward. It's where they put the loony-tunes. Doze and I snuck up there once on a dare from Boog. We always joke about it, as in, "Where did you escape from? The fifth floor? Ha ha." No joke today. Because that's where Aunt Daphne is.

I still can't believe it because it's so bizarre. That kind of stuff happens to other people, never to you. But it must happen to practically everybody sooner or later, because the place is full. You could hardly take a step without bumping into someone shuffling along with their eyes glazed over. It's not the kind of thing you want to climb on top of buildings and shout about, that you have a friend there, or a relative. There's no question about that. I guess people just want to keep quiet about it.

Mom and Dad and I are in the car. We're quiet. We're nervous. We don't know what to expect. I look at Mom out of the corner of my eye. She's looking straight ahead. The end of her nose is red like she's getting a cold. Now she knows I'm looking at her. She looks away, then right at me. There is a sudden itch in my right eye. I rub it and look straight ahead. It's funny how those itches come like that. Dad doesn't say anything either. If this was yesterday, he'd be blabbing away about something just to fill the air. But he's quiet now too.

We pull up in the hospital loading zone where there's a black half-ton in front of us with double smoke stacks sticking up beside the cab. There are two guys sitting in the truck wearing baseball caps. Their hair sticks out from under these caps and needs cutting. Preferably with a lawn mower. Because on the tail-gate of their truck, there's a bumper-sticker and it says, "Suicide is fun." We all just sit there for about three days staring at this.

Finally Dad sort of shakes his head and says, "Let's go."

We get out and go up the steps. There's only five of them, but it seems like fifty.

The commissionaire gives us the once over like he's trying to decide if I'm old enough to be there. You have to be twelve. We go straight to the elevator and there's a woman standing there in her housecoat. She's attached to a bottle that's hanging from a kind of metal tree on wheels. When the door opens, she pushes her tree in front of her and one of the wheels gets stuck in the crack between the inside of elevator and the rest of the world. She gives it a shove and the whole thing just about tumbles backwards onto us. But I catch it, help her straighten it out, and we all get onto the elevator.

"Thanks," she says. "What floor?"

"Five," I say. I am secretly hoping that the elevator will plunge, hurtling us all to the bottom of the shaft. It's only one floor, but it would be a good excuse not to go through with this. I stare at the numbers above the door. That's what you're supposed to do. You collect yourselves, stand in a nice little group and stare at the numbers.

At least that's what most people do. But not Dad. He gets very uncomfortable in elevators and feels he has to talk. He gives the woman the once over. She has a large bandage around the lower part of her left leg. "What's in the bottle?" he asks.

"Vodka," the woman says.

"Vodka?" says Dad.

"I asked for Scotch, but they gave me vodka." She doesn't even crack a smile.

And while the elevator stops at the third floor, the woman gets off with her vodka tree and just about wipes out the nurse who gets on. The nurse stares at the numbers.

"Weird," says Dad.

The nurse sort of looks at him.

"Not you," says Dad, "the woman with the vodka."

Now the nurse takes a good look at Dad and says, "What?"

164 YULETIDE BLUES

"Oh, nothing," says Dad, who looks at me, then Mom. I look at the nurse, and the nurse looks at me. Then she looks at Mom and Dad. Mom and Dad look at the nurse. Then we all look at the numbers. The numbers blink. Five.

The elevator stops. We all get out.

I don't know what I am expecting, but whatever it is, this is not it. Everything looks normal. Every*body* looks normal. And you know they can't be, or they wouldn't be here — unless everybody's visiting. The only thing a little bit off is there's piano music playing somewhere. Classical piano, that very boring stuff that some people think is so great. People like Aunt Florence.

Mom grabs my arm and says, "This way." For some reason I am heading left towards the piano music and didn't look at the wall which has numbers on it, 519-537, and an arrow pointing right. Mom is still hanging onto my arm. Then she grabs Dad's too. "What are we going to say?" she asks.

"I don't know," says Dad.

I am still thinking about how normal the people look. The thing about people is they look fine on the outside. But the next thing you know, they're dead. That's one kind of people. And then of course there's the other kind, the kind who look like their faces are on inside out and backwards, or they have no hands or legs or something, but they hum along just fine, thank you, like nothing's wrong at all. And they live forever. Well, maybe not forever, but they don't roll over and die because of the way they look.

"Everybody looks fine," I say.

"Sh-sh," Mom says, "this is it." Five-twenty-nine. The door is partially closed.

Suddenly, panic hits me. I stop cold. Mom and Dad almost get yanked off their feet. Like we're playing crack-the-whip.

"What's the matter?" Mom says. As if she doesn't know.

"I don't want to go in."

"Why?"

"What if she's . . . ?" What if she's what? I don't know, I'm afraid.

"We're here. Let's go. Come on." And she drags me half-way through the door.

Of course I can't let Aunt Daph see her dragging me, so I go of my own accord and make this jaunty nothing's-wrong and oh-what-a-coincidence-to-see-you-here entrance. I can be such a jerk sometimes.

And there she is, lying on the bed, plugged into one of those vodka trees. Her eyes are closed. As she hears us enter, she opens them, turns and smiles. She looks . . . fine. I mean, she does not look like somebody who just tried to cash it in. No bandages across her skull.

No bullet holes. Fine. Why is she smiling?

"Hi," she says.

"Hi," we say in unison.

Aunt Daph's got the window bed. The bed next to her is empty, but messy. Whoever it belongs to is out of the room.

"Nice room," I say.

"Yeah," she says, "but the woman next to me is a real fruitcake."

We nod. "You're looking okay," I say.

"So are you," says Aunt Daph. We laugh a little because this is a joke.

Then we stand there like bumps on a log, even though everybody knows what everybody else is thinking. *How did she do it?*

"They pumped out my stomach," says Aunt Daph. "They stuck a tube down through me and sucked everything out. It hurts like hell."

She did it with pills. She knows exactly what we're thinking.

"Yes, I cleaned out the medicine cabinet." She has stopped smiling and is looking out the window.

"Why?" says Mom.

"Because I didn't have a gun," says Aunt Daph.

"You should have called us," says Dad.

"Oh, do you have one?" she looks at Dad.

"You know what I mean," he says.

"I'm tired of calling for help. Tired, tired, tired, tired. I'm tired and I'm alone. You can't help that. No one can help that. But me."

There's no snappy comeback to a statement like that. I mean, you want to say something, but you can't.

"Well, who found you?" asks Mom. She's trying to get at the fact that maybe she's not alone as she thinks.

"Nobody found me. I chickened out. I don't even have the courage to kill myself. I called 9-1-1." She really is alone.

"That's good," says Dad. "Sometimes it takes more courage to live than it does to die. You're a strong, beautiful person. It hurts to see you so unhappy." He takes her hand, and squeezes it. Aunt Daph just looks out the window. It is not much of a view, though. In fact, it's a shitty view, but the window is large and lets in lots of light. It looks out over the hospital power plant and piece of a parking lot. I can see a black truck in the lot. I wonder if it's the same one we saw going in, with the sign on the bumper.

Suddenly Aunt Daph turns and looks me straight in the eye. She locks me there like a rabbit in headlights.

"I'm sorry Lanny, you were going to stay with me," she says and keeps me there for a second or two, then turns them off, turns away and lets me go.

I don't know why I've come. I'm visiting someone I don't know. I want to leave now. I am not looking at Aunt Daphne anymore but someone else, someone who is very, very old and very, very tired. I realize that I am a complete idiot, a child, a frightened rabbit. I am now ready to go.

But Grandma and Grandpa arrive. They hug and stuff, and everybody tries to be nice. "How's the food?" Grandma says.

Food. She wants to know how the food is. I can't believe it.

"I don't know. I haven't eaten yet. They've got me plugged into this." And she raises his arm an inch.

"Vodka?" Dad says.

"I wish," says Daphne. "It's sugar water or something. They pretty well drained me and now they're trying to put some back I guess."

"When are you going to get out?" asks Grandpa.

"I don't know. A couple of days. They want to do an *assessment.*"

"Well, when you're done, you stay home with us. We'll take care of you," says Grandma.

A silence fills the room, and Aunt Daphne looks out the window again. There are stories about people pitching themselves out through the windows here. I wonder if she is thinking that. I wonder if they've put nets below. But if somebody really wants to do it, I guess they'll do it no matter what. There is so much I want to know about Aunt Daph but I'm afraid to ask.

I excuse myself and step out into the corridor. I want to get away and let them talk about whatever it is they want to talk about, boring adult talk. My feet are moving, carrying me along with them. I can hear the piano again. My feet stop. I'm standing in front of the elevator. I decide I'll wait here.

The piano music is getting louder. No, it's not getting louder, it's coming closer to me. It just *seems* like it's getting louder. I edge around the corner, and sure enough, there is a little old lady in a wheelchair with a cassette deck on her lap. She's slowly wheeling down the corridor with this piano music playing in front of her. She looks at me and she very slowly smiles, just like Aunt Daph did when we came into her room. I turn away, towards the elevator doors just as they open.

And who should get off but the woman with the vodka tree.

"Hi," she says, "you still here?"

"Yeah," I say.

"What are you in for?" she asks.

"Oh, I'm just waiting."

"Yeah," she says. "Me too." And she walks away pushing her tree in front of her.

I watch her go up the corridor, and without looking at me she waves, over her shoulder, and takes a sharp right into Aunt Daphne's room.

I have a definite urge to go back, not to visit Aunt Daph, but to find out more about this weird woman. My feet have the same urge, because I find they're carrying me that way. It suddenly occurs to me that I am nuts and everyone around me is sane. I know nothing and everybody around me knows too much, and if someone was to stop me right now, I couldn't prove who I am, or who I think I am.

I walk back into the room and everyone is huddled around Aunt Daph's bed like she was a quarterback calling a play. I get closer and see that they are all looking at a stone Aunt Daph has on her lap. "... but now it's brighter. It's definitely getting brighter," Aunt Daph is saying.

"What is?" says a voice from the corner of the room. It's the woman, sitting on a chair beside her bed, vodka tree and all. We all look at her. "Just curious," she says.

"My *life stone*," says Aunt Daph, holding it up. "It's getting brighter."

"Oh yeah, well, as long as they leave the curtains open it'll stay bright too," says the woman. She smiles at me. I look at her leg with the bandage on it.

"It's an infection. Do you want to see it?"

I shake my head no.

"It's nothing much to look at. It's just a little hole in my leg. They think it's psychosomatic, but this is supposed to clear it up," she says, tapping the vodka tree thing.

I go from feeling nuts a few minutes ago, to feeling totally sane. My problems are nothing compared to these, I mean, when you consider Aunt Daph's suicide attempt and *life stones*, along with this other woman's unreal hole in her leg. Still, I have this funny feeling they're going to be friends.

We leave pretty soon after this and as we're going home in the car, things are pretty quiet. To say this put a crimp in the parents' get-away plans is to understate things a bit.

I might get to go after all. However, I seriously doubt it, because Mom and Dad have just started fighting.

I hate it when Mom and Dad fight. I hate it worse when they fight about me. And I absolutely positively hate it the most when they fight about me *when I'm there and they act as if I'm not!*

Like, I'm sitting there, and they refer to me as "he":

"Well, he can't go to your mother's because they're going to be too busy with Daphne," says Mom.

"So?" says Dad.

"It's too much to ask. He'll get in the way."

"He won't get in the way," says Dad.

"If he won't get in the way, he'll be neglected. And your father's going in for that knee operation."

"Can't we send him to Kelowna? To your parents?"

"No," says Mom. "And it's too late even if it wasn't no. Why don't we take him?"

(Yes, take him.)

"We can't afford to take him."

"Well then, maybe we should just stay home!"

"Fine. You can stay home with him, I'll go!"

(This is a low blow, and now things really get ugly.)

"What about your Aunt Florence?"

(See?)

"She's too old to look after him."

"She's not too old. He's not a baby."

(Thanks, Mom.)

"Well . . ."

"Aunt Florence's?" I say, out loud.

"You keep out of this. This doesn't concern you!"

If it doesn't concern me, who does it concern?

Chapter eighteen

I'm at G.O.D.'s, the Grand Old Dame's, Aunt Florence's. This is where I am going to spend the next ten days of my life, which goes to prove that life is hell. Worse than hell. At least in hell there's something to do, shovelling coal or something. But at Aunt Florence's there is nothing. Nothing. Great vast yawns of nothing but a cat and old lady's things. This is where I am. I've died and been sent to hell.

I've been here twenty minutes and already I'm covered with cat hair. I think of violins. Shawna likes cats. She has two of them and says they're very smart. She also says they're like humans would be if they could get away with it. Sure. If this cat is so smart, what's it doing here? Waiting to be a violin.

But what am I going to do for ten days? I don't even have school, it's Christmas break. Thank God I've got a hockey game tonight. I've got four games and two practices, that's six things to do in ten days. Other than that, nothing. I have to take a cab to the rink. It'll cost a fortune too, because she lives way out here in the boonies. I don't know anybody around here, nothing! This is me screaming. Hear it?

174 YULETIDE BLUES

Nothing. I can't even scream. I'll wake up the cat. I hate cats.

The last thing Mom said to me before the both of them whisked off to the moon was this:

"Try and be nice."

I hope her baggage falls off the plane. I hope she loses her old bathing suit and has to wear her new one. I hope it rains. I hope it snows. "Try and be nice." Of course I'll try and be nice! What else can you be to an old lady in a wheelchair? I'll take it out on the cat. Later.

First you have to get a picture of this place. Think green, jungle green. You practically got to hack your way across the living room it's so full of plants. And it smells like a swamp, without the bugs. I bet the cat loves this place.

Along the walls, the green walls, are shelves. And on the shelves are books. There must be a million books in this place. We don't have this many books in the school library. How can one person read so many books? Maybe the plants read them. Maybe the cat reads them. And as if that wasn't bad enough, they're all in *German!*

In the middle of all this is a piano. Not just any rinky dink little house piano, but a very big, large, *grand* piano. It's the kind of thing you see in concert halls, on a very large stage, *not* in your Aunt Florence's living room, surrounded by books and plants. How do the plants stand it? How does the cat stand it?

Nowhere in this room is there any sign of the twentieth century, except for electric lights and a fire extinguisher. She has a thing about them. There's one in every room. But back in the living room, there's no TV, no VCR, no stereo, forget the computer, there's not even a radio. Nothing . . . Okay, there's a phone, the first one they ever made. A black thing that weighs a ton that you have to dial, on a little stand right next to the grand piano. Throw in a couple of chairs covered in cat hair and that's it.

So when you go into the kitchen and you expect to see a wood stove and a couple of dead chickens dangling from the ceiling, you get a real shock. It looks like the flight deck of the Star Ship *Enterprise*. You half expect R2D2 to waltz in and pour you a glass of milk. But he doesn't. You have to get it yourself out of this fridge that's about the size of the grand piano on its side. It's loaded too. How does one person eat all that food? Maybe the plants eat it. Maybe the cat eats it.

Everything is state of the art in this kitchen. It's small, but boy, is it crammed full. There's slicers, toasters, ovens, choppers, grinders, things I've never seen before and tools hanging all over the white walls.

The sink is something else. It's u-shaped stainless steel in the corner and has about fourteen taps sticking out of it. Okay, I exaggerate, it only has three taps, but there's a dishwasher underneath and a plant above, hanging in the window. For some reason I feel sorry for the one lonely plant, above the sink.

Anyway, Aunt Florence has told me to help myself so I'm at the fridge collecting ice cubes from the coin return slot (that's what it looks like) when this *sound* happens. I drop a dozen ice cubes all over the floor. You can't hear the ice cubes fall, that's how big the sound is. And the sound continues. It's the piano.

About the same time I drop the ice cubes, the cat comes skittering into the kitchen, slides through the cubes trying to stop, then disappears into a little hole between the fridge and the cupboard. I don't know why, but I suddenly like this cat. It's stupid but it's doing what I would like to do. Hiding. I now see what Shawna means.

I never knew a piano could be so loud. I peer around the corner into the living room. There sits Aunt Florence. She has rolled herself up to the piano and is playing a thunderstorm. I can't hear music, I just expect rain to come down. You got to be deaf to appreciate this. She sees me and stops.

"Do you like it?" she asks.

"It's loud," I say, trying to be nice.

"It's Beethowen," she says, "he vas deaf."

"He was lucky."

"Oh, you'll get used to it. Villy did."

Villy is the cat. It's probably actually Willy. She gets her "v's" and "w's" mixed up. Willy is not deaf.

"He's behind the fridge," I say.

"Yes, from there he likes to listen."

I nod. What else can I do? She starts playing again. I want to join Willy behind the fridge. Instead, I go to "my" room. It's very small and green and does not have a water bed. It has a table, a chair, and a cot. There is a small picture of some guy fishing on the wall. The window has snow outside to match the white curtains. That's it. Nothing else.

I close the door and listen to the muffled rainstorm in the living room. I look at the guy fishing and wonder what he's doing there on Aunt Florence's wall. He looks back at me and wonders the same thing. I tell him, "My parents left me here." He doesn't answer me. I don't even know the guy and already I think he's a fink. This would be a good time to unpack. I unpack. There's no place to put anything so I just leave it in the bag, except for Jack the penguin and my ghetto. I put on a tape, *Minglewood*. Guess what? The damn thing doesn't work! Nothing! What else can go wrong?

Chapter nineteen

I go about three hours early to the hockey game, not because I'm particularly anxious to run into Boog but because I'm bored to death. I sit around and watch a game of peewees. One kid thinks he's Wayne Gretzky. He's wearing ninety-nine and everything. He even has one side of his sweater tucked in. He's pretty good too, but I bet all his team-mates hate him because he thinks he's good. He's a puck hog and while he's dipsy-doodling around the ice, this big kid from the other team comes along and creams him. Everybody cheers. He's hurt and nobody helps him up, till finally the ref blows the whistle and play stops. Everybody gathers around him but nobody does anything. He eventually gets up and then starts chasing the big guy with his stick, but the linesman grabs him and they throw him out of the game. "Good," I think. Meanwhile, there's a lot of yelling by some old broad who's probably Gretzky's mother, and when he gets off the ice and walks by me, Mother's right there too, gabbing away like nobody's business. "You should have hit him. You should have clobbered him," she's saying. They should ban mothers like that. But the kid turns, takes off his helmet, and says very politely, "Mother, would you please shut your mouth?" There's tears in his eyes.

I bet he quits hockey real soon.

Not me, it's all I've got to live for right now.

I head towards the dressing room, dragging my gear behind me. Boog is always the first one there. I know it's going to be him and me alone. This should be interesting. I screw up my courage.

I open the door.

No Boog.

In his place is Brad, our backup. "Hi, Lan," he says.

"Where's Boog?" I ask.

"He's been called up. Petey's been hurt." Petey's the starter for the Junior A team in town. So Boog is the back-up goalie to their back-up. "I finally get a chance to start." He's excited and I'm confused.

"How come good things happen to such jerks?"

"What?" says Brad.

"Not you — Boog."

"He's not a jerk, he just got into some trouble. He's a good goalie."

"He's a jerk," I say. I don't go into the details. I suppose from Boog's point of view I'm a jerk. So maybe we're even. It's still not fair though. I mean, Howcome bad things happen to good people, like Aunt Daph, and good things happen to jerks, like Boog? "I hope he breaks a leg," I add.

We're playing the Mohawks. Again. Why are things always so intense with these guys? I mean you'd think this was the Stanley Cup or something. Anyway, we're down two to one and it's half-way through the third. I'm not playing well. I'm tight. I just can't get loose. I've missed at least three good shots, one of them with their goalie down. The Mohawks are up to their usual crap, cheap shots, intimidation. And they're such a bunch of whiners.

We've got them locked in their end and the pressure's on. They're trying to squeeze the puck up the boards but I pinch in. I can't get it with my stick, so I kick. While my foot is in the air, I get hit. I go down. My stick goes up. Something cracks. I can see my stick is fine. It's my leg. Fade to black.

You can't believe the pain of breaking your leg until it happens to you. It's enough to make you black out, which is exactly what I do for a moment or two and the next thing I know they're sliding me onto a stretcher. Brad our backup goalie has come over beside me and he says two words.

"Wrong leg," he says. For a moment I don't know what he means, then it occurs to me.

"Oh yeah, very wrong leg." It was supposed to be Boog's.

I don't know if you've ever had to go to the hospital when your parents are out of town, but let me tell you, it's absolutely no fun at all. Nobody can find my hospitalization number and all that sort of stuff, plus the fact they need permission to fix me from a parent or guardian, who in this case is Aunt Florence who doesn't answer the phone for half an hour because she's most likely playing the piano again and can't hear it. Eventually they do get hold of her and our family doctor who probably has to swear on a stack of bibles that I'm who I'm supposed to be. In the meantime, the coach is keeping me company, trying to crack jokes about the whole situation till it stops being funny.

It's getting close to midnight by the time I get X-rayed and now I'm just lying in this little curtained-off bed staring at the ceiling waiting for them to put the cast on. The coach is out in the waiting room. I'm sort of groggy from the pain killers they've given me, and suddenly I get this strange feeling. It's as though I can see through five floors above me through the ceiling and there's Aunt Daphne. It has just occurred to me that we are in the same building. I no sooner think that thought when the curtain beside me rustles. I look. No one's there.

182 YULETIDE BLUES

I'm alone. I am truly alone. There is me in this room, in this town, in this country, on this continent, in this hemisphere, on this planet, in this galaxy, in this universe, in these universes. And this is when I start crying. I can't help it. I sob like a baby. Aunt Daph is alone, I am alone, everyone is alone. The buffalo is alone. I know what Aunt Daph has tried and others have done. There are no *Things of a Higher Order* and if you think there are, you are just kidding yourself because you are really nothing and nothing matters because you are alone. And this is what Aunt Daph feels, only a thousand times worse. I cry for her here tonight. I am alone.

"Are you all right, dear?" The curtain rustles again. It's a nurse.

"It doesn't matter," I sob.

"Can I get something for you?" she asks.

"It doesn't matter," I sob some more.

"Yes, it does, dear — *everything* matters."

"No, it doesn't," I sob. I'm doing a lot of sobbing.

She puts her hand on my forehead and pushes back my hair. "The doctor will be here in a minute to put your cast on. You just *stay here.*"

This strikes me as kind of funny in the midst of all my doom and gloom. I half laugh through my sobs, "Where the heck am I going to go?"

She smiles and pushes back my hair again and leaves. I am no longer alone.

The doctor comes in, a small Pakistani guy with twinkly eyes, and shows me the X-rays, explaining that something called the tibia is broken. "I very much like fixing things," he says and starts putting on the cast. He's like a kindergarten kid playing with plaster moulds. He's having a ball.

After he's done, I have to wait a while longer for the plaster to get hard, and the nurse asks if there's anything I want.

"I want to see my aunt," I say.

"Your aunt?"

"She's on the fifth floor. She tried to commit suicide," I say.

"Well, it's pretty late now," says the nurse, "she's probably asleep."

"I know. I still want to see her. I want to see if she's alive."

The nurse sort of looks around the room, as though she's hearing voices, and says, "I'll be back in minute."

She comes back with a wheelchair, helps me into it and takes me through a maze of hallways, up the elevator and onto the fifth floor. I tell her the room number. My heart is pounding. She says something to another nurse who's behind a counter. The other nurse looks at me and nods.

184 YULETIDE BLUES

We go to the room.

There on her bed, beneath the moonlight shining through the window, is Aunt Daph, sleeping. She looks like an angel. I whisper to the nurse, "Do you have some paper?"

I write a little note and put it on her bed.

It says, "I love you. Lanny."

Chapter twenty

It's a couple days later. Aunt Daph has called and thanked me for the note. She says she starts her therapy today, and she feels fine physically, but she hopes they take her off the drugs she's on. She says she can't concentrate and she rambles on a bit. I tell her about my leg and we promise to talk again soon.

In the meantime, I stink. I smell like something the dog dragged in. I really need a bath.

Have you ever tried to take a bath with a cast on your leg? Don't. It can't be done. Well, it *can*, but if anybody ever walks in on you, or *rolls* in on you like happened to me, it's pretty embarrassing. I'm naked, except for the cast and a sponge, and I get stuck sitting sideways in the tub and can't get out. I call for help. In rolls Aunt Florence. She doesn't laugh. She smiles. You don't want to hear about it, but between the two of us, we manage to get me out. Do you think I can show my face around here? Now? Forget it. To top it off, I don't have anything that will fit over the cast. So I wear my hockey pants. It's the only thing I can do.

I have to eat. I hobble into the kitchen. The piano's playing. Willy is in his hiding-place.

I open the fridge and knock one crutch out from under me. I grab to keep from falling but end up taking a litre of milk with me, all over the floor. The piano keeps playing. I clean up and the cat comes out to help.

Later, I try reading. Or I should say, I try looking for a book. I have to do something. This stops Aunt Florence playing the piano. Silence. It's amazing how she can get around in that thing — the wheelchair. She's quiet and fast. Zoom, she's there.

"Vut are you looking for?"

"Something to read. In English." I still find it hard to look at her directly, because she's *seen* me. You know. But it sounds like she wants to talk. We've never really done that.

"Anysing in mind?" she says.

"No," I say. Something with lots of pictures. "Got any, like, hockey novels or anything?"

"I don't sink so."

Think. Sink. "Where'd you get all these books anyway?"

"I buy sem. Some are qvite dreadful, but I like seir company. Books und plants make vonderful varm company ven you're alone."

"Oh yeah?" This is news to me. I notice my father the poet's books. All three of them, slim volumes of poetry. I have never read them. There's *Fiona's Sky*, *West Wind Why* and *Fake*. *Fake* looks promising, I mean as far as titles go.

But there's not even a picture on the cover, just a design. It's his latest. At least they're in English. I pull it down.

"I sink sat is his best," she says, "Alsough I like some of *Fiona's Sky* too."

"I've never read it," I say.

"You should," she says. "It vould be a vonderful start. Who knows, maybe someday you could write like sat too."

Whoopee.

"I doubt it."

I read *Fiona's Sky*. Not the whole thing, just parts. It's all about the sky, from all kinds of points of view. I read one called "Buffalo Sky".

> A huge grey rock
> The size of Grandma's living room
> Fell off a glacier
> Plunk onto the valley floor
> Settling jagged and alone
> Till the buffalo came
> And over eons glazed it smooth
> Lodging tufts of fur in frost cracks.
> But long before they built the dam,
> The buffalo were shot,
> Their quintessence passing to the cosmos.
> Till now with the valley flooded
> The rock itself lay full fathom five
> And I lay face up
> Buried in the prairie sun
> And watch the white buffalo
> Billow in the sky.

So this is what he writes. And you know what? My father is a thief. That's *me* lying outside in the last verse. It was on Grandma's front lawn when I was about six. I'm lying there and I say, "Hey Dad, that cloud looks like a buffalo!" And that line about the rock being the size of Grandma's living room, I know the living room he's talking about. He uses my clouds and Grandma's living room to make his poem. That's how he makes them, he steals things. And I still don't get it, I mean, so what? I'd have to study it in school to understand it.

I put the book back.

"Aren't you going to read it?"

"The whole book?"

"Yes."

"Nah. It's too . . . I don't understand it."

"You should try to understand it. Sat's vut makes it fun."

"Fun?" This is not my idea of a good time. In my worst dreams this is not my idea of fun. This woman does not know what fun is. "I think it's like beyond my depths, you know?"

"I see," she says. "Try sis," and takes down this old book that is battered and bruised and has seen better days. It's called *Treasure Island*, written by a guy named Robert Louis Stevenson.

"Looks old," I say.

"It is. It's even older than me."

"How old are you?"

"Never ask a voman her age, young man. It's not done."

"Sorry." Try and be nice.

"That's qvite all right." And she wheels off into the kitchen.

I am so bored, I actually read *Treasure Island*. It takes me two days. It's about this kid, Jim Hawkins, who ends up going treasure-hunting with a bunch of pirates. He doesn't *mean* to, but that's what happens. And one of them, Long John Silver, has only got one leg. I sort of relate to him. He's also got a two hundred-year-old parrot attached to his shoulder who says "Pieces of eight!" all the time. All I've got is Jack the Penguin who doesn't say anything. Anyway, in the end, they find the treasure and everybody gets their just desserts. I thought I'd never get through it, but to tell you the truth, it'd probably make a pretty good movie.

During the time I'm reading, old Aunt Florence has been feeding me pretty well. She disappears into the *Enterprise* and comes out with all kinds of interesting food. She gets supplies from some guy who delivers her groceries once a week, I guess. That's what she tells me. I haven't seen him yet.

She has also been playing the piano. She asks me where I am in the book, and she starts playing. And whatever it is, it sort of goes along with what I'm reading. It's kind of neat, like the music in a movie goes along with what you're seeing. You don't always notice it, but it's always there.

I have to change my mind a little bit about the piano playing. I can see why the plants like it. And since I'm turning into a bit of a vegetable myself, I have to admit I'm getting used to it. After you get over how annoying it is, it can be very soothing — loud, but soothing. The only major problem is that the phone is right next to the piano. So go ahead, try make a phone call with a piano blasting in your ear. I mean, you can't turn it down — the piano. I've tried calling Shawna a couple times, because she's supposed to be back today. No luck. Which is just as well because she wouldn't have been able to hear me anyway.

I'm actually reading another book. This one is called *Kidnapped* and it's by the same guy who wrote *Treasure Island*. So far it's not as good, but maybe it's because Aunt Florence isn't playing the piano as much. In fact, she's hardly playing at all today. She seems to be getting ready for something, like, I mean, she's got these curlers in her hair and has spent a lot of time fussing around in the bathroom. I hobble over.

"What are you doing?" I might as well come straight to the point.

"Getting ready." I was right.

"For what?"

"Vell, I'm expecting a caller sis evening."

"A caller?" This just blurts out of me.

"Vut you vould call a date."

"A date? You're going on a date? At your age?"

"You don't know how old I am." This is true. She turns to me and she is experimenting with make-up. "How do I look?"

"Good." Try and be nice. "You look, just as good as you can look." I mean, really.

"Goot," she says. But I can't just leave it hang here.

"So . . . what are you going to do?"

"Ve're going to a concert."

"A concert?"

"Yashamouri is playing. He is wery goot."

"Oh . . . What does he play?"

"Lanny, he plays piano." I should have known.

"Are you going in the wheelchair?"

"Certainly. How else?"

Yes, of course, how stupid of me. I can't get over it. The old girl is going on a date.

So after supper, she takes the curlers out of her hair and puts on a blue dress with little flowers all over it. She looks quite, well, I want to say pretty, but that's not it. She looks like you can tell she was pretty when she was about fifty years younger. I don't tell her this, but it's the truth. And the other thing is, she's actually nervous. You can see it. She's trying to remember if she's forgotten anything and then has me climb with my bum leg to the top of a closet to get this black leather purse. Once she gets that, she figures she's ready and then sits back to wait. But she's not very good at waiting. This guy, whoever it is, isn't due for another half hour so she goes to the piano and starts playing this really strange tune. She plays it very softly. Even the cat, Willy, sticks around to hear this one. I didn't know the piano could make such soft noise. Suddenly I recognize the tune. It's "Silent Night". I've never heard it played like that before, and just past the point I recognize what it is, she stops. She stops and sits there.

"How come you stopped?"

"I try. I try to play it all, but I can't."

"Why?" I mean, she can play *anything*.

"It's a long story. You vould find it uninteresting."

Now she's got me. Even if it's uninteresting, I'm interested.

"You can't just stop and say I wouldn't be interested."

"It vas long before you vere born. It vas in the var. I vas just a young girl. I vas not older much san you." And she stops, either to think about how she should tell me, or to dismiss the whole idea.

I don't know much about her past. I only know that she and my grandparents came here after the war from Germany. I guess there were some pretty heavy times, with a lot of killing and concentration camps and things like that. Some of the guys I know at school are totally into the war. I mean, they know all sorts of things that happened and they, like, make a study of planes and guns and stuff. It's kind of like some other guys who are into baseball cards and can tell you the stats of the winning team of the 1934 World Series. But the guys who are into war can tell you what kind of plane it is just by the shadow it shows against a night sky. Why they bother about it, I don't know. But it's not the same as being there, and I got to admit now I'm curious.

"Yeah, so . . . you were my age, and then what?"

"I vas wery goot pianist ven I vas young."

"You still are," I say. She's the best piano player I know, even though I don't much care for what she plays.

"No, I vas *very* good." She actually pronounces the "v" this time. "Ant I play concert, I play lots of concerts ewen during the var in Berlin. One night ve play concert, it is Christmas,- *Weihnachten*, ant ve hear varning sat bombs are coming. But bombs are alvays coming now. So ve play anyvay. Ve don't sink about it, ve just play. And ve play *'Stille Nacht'*, 'Silent Night', and vhile ve are playing . . . "

"You get bombed," I say, thinking I got the drift, but realize that "getting bombed" has other meanings. I quickly add, "A bomb hits."

"Yes, a bomb hit very close, but ve keep playing. Ve do not stop now. Ve play louder, ant so loud to not hear the bombs. Ant soon they stop." So does Aunt Flo.

"Is that it?"

"Ant ve go outside. Cold, I am vearing mitts for my hands. Ant sere are fires in se houses. Ant ve hear people scream in se houses. I see a little boy. I see him at a vindow. I go to help him out, to pull him srough se vindow. He is burning. Vat he is vearing is on fire. Ant I put out se fire. But he is dead now. He is liwing and now he is dead. I don't know why. I feel sen my hand. I take off my mitt. It is burnt and it is vet. I look at my hand . . . " And as she says this, she holds up her hand. She has beautiful hands, with long fingers, but when she turns her palm out, I see a small scar below her thumb. It doesn't look like much.

"Ant se vet is blood. My hand is all blood. Ant I cannot close my hand. Some glass, I guess, in se vindow I pull se boy from. It's not big cut, but enough. I can't play piano, somesing cut sere, I can't play piano. *Weihnachten*, nineteen-forty-sree."

"But you play, I mean, you play now."

"Oh yes, after many years, I play a little. But not like before."

This bit of information sort of slows the conversation, if you want to call it that. It's been pretty much a monologue. Anyway, it slows to a dead stop. I never knew this. And I never heard Aunt Florence talk like this before either. You never think of old people as having pasts. They're just people you know who are old. But they have things that have happened to them, making them what they are. Old. How one little scar on her thumb can mean all that. And here I am sitting with a broken leg. Fifty years from now, when I'm talking to my great nephew or niece or whatever, will I limp? Will I ever be able to play hockey again? I mean really play, like in the pros? The thought scares me. I don't want to think about it.

I change the subject.

"So who's this guy you're going out with tonight?"

"Mr. Stewens. He is taking me."

"Who is he?"

"A friend. Ve meet, ve met," she corrects herself, "last year at se auction. Monty."

"He's a Mountie?"

"No, Monty, sat's his name, Monty."

"That's good," I say.

"Vat?"

"That you have a friend that will take you places." And it is. I mean you, don't think of Aunt Flo going places, doing things, and certainly not with men. I figure, "Jeez, there's life in the old girl yet."

I build this mental image of Mr. Stevens. He's a Mountie, with grey hair. Big.

And right on cue, the doorbell rings.

He blows my image right away. Mr. Stevens is practically a midget. And old — he looks older than Aunt Florence. Because I answer the door wearing my hockey pants and a cast, he looks at me kind of funny. I smile as though everything is normal and invite him into the living room. I guess he's been here before, because he walks ahead of me like he knows where he's going, but when he gets to the doorway of living room, he stops like he ran into a wall. I almost knock him over because I don't expect him to stop so soon.

"Hello, Monty," Aunt Florence says.

"Hello, Florence," says Monty, Mr. Stevens.

"Vould you care for some tea before ve go?"

And here there is a pause. Monty looks stunned.

"What, what happened?"

"Ven?"

"You're in a wheelchair."

"Yes, vell, I fell you see."

"Why didn't you tell me?"

"Vell, I did, I told you about it."

"No, no, you didn't mention it."

"It's nosing. Do you vant tea?"

"It's twenty below. Outside."

"Yes, it is."

"You didn't tell me you were in a wheelchair."

It is suddenly about twenty below inside too, like everything is frozen. You get the distinct impression that Mr. Midget Stevens is unhappy about Aunt Florence's wheelchair. At this particular moment, Willy the cat wanders into the room. He walks over to Mr. Stevens and rubs up against his leg. Why do cats always do that? Especially to people you know don't like them? Mr. Stevens sort of shoves Willy away with his foot.

"Please don't kick se cat," says Aunt Florence.

"I can't take you in a wheelchair," says Monty Stevens.

"Cats do not like to be kicked."

"I can't take you."

"Vhy not?"

"I didn't *kick* the cat. I *moved* it, with my foot."

The conversation seems to be out of sync here. I try to get it back on track.

"If anybody would like tea, I'll go put the water on," I say, and I make three-legged tracks through the jungle into the kitchen. It's times like this that I'm an amazing coward. But I listen.

"So you don't vant to take me."

"I do Florence, I just don't think it's possible."

"Anysing is possible, if you vant it. Because I'm in a vheelchair is no reason for not going to se concert. Ant it's no reason to kick my cat."

"I did not kick your cat, Florence. I'm not as young as I used to be, I can't go throwing wheelchairs around . . ."

I turn on one of the taps. And can't hear anymore. I really don't want to listen. I fill up the tea kettle. This takes about thirty seconds. I dump out the kettle and fill it up again just to take more time. Officially I tell myself I'm rinsing it. I think I hear the door slam. I turn off the tap.

There is silence. He must be gone. Or dead. Maybe they're both dead. Or both gone.

"Does anybody want tea?" I call. No answer. I hobble to the living room.

And there, sitting there in a blue dress with white flowers, in a wheelchair, is a little girl. There are tears in her eyes.

"What's wrong?" I ask.

And the little girl turns into Aunt Florence.

"I'm too olt," she says, and drags the word "old" out real long, and her voice is quavering.

I don't know what to say, so I say the wrong thing.

"Maybe you should have warned him."

"Sat's no excuse. Sat's no excuse for him to come here ant kick my cat! If he vants to kick cats, he can kick his own cat. But he's not coming here and kick my cat ant tell me I'm too old! I'm sixty-eight! I'm sixty-eight years olt — if sat's too olt to go to a concert in a vheelchair, sen I should be dead! Shoot me, I should be *dead!*"

"Don't say that."

"I am alone, I should be dead!"

"You're not alone, I'm here."

"You don't vant to be here vit me, no one vants . . ." She doesn't continue. I am stunned. She is right. I don't want to be there. I suddenly feel guilty. If I had stepped in and done something when Mr. Stevens was here, if they had gone out, this wouldn't be happening. But it's too late. I thought I was doing the right thing. Now I'm just as guilty as him.

She has turned and rolled herself to the piano. She starts playing, quiet at first, but soon building to a loud storm. Then she just starts banging on the keys and banging. Something's going to break!

"Stop! Don't, Aunt Florence! Stop!" I touch her shoulder.

She turns on me like lightning and with her arm extended she hits me in the side of the head with the back of her hand. This knocks me off-balance, and I fall.

Chapter twenty-one

The piano is still humming and I'm looking up at her. I'm not hurt, just stunned. She looks at me, her mouth open, like she's amazed at what she's done. I think we're both amazed. And all she does is shake her head a little bit, "no". Then rolls into her room.

For some reason I think this is all my fault and I go to her door and stand there staring at my cast, trying to think of something sensible to say.

"I'm sorry," I say.

Nothing.

"I'm sorry, Aunt Florence, please come out."

Still nothing.

I decide I better just leave her alone for awhile. I go to bed. This ends day four at Aunt Flo's house.

* * *

I don't know if you've ever spent any time in a house with a cat and an old woman who won't come out of her room, but after a time you start wondering if people are dead and that sort of thing. I mean, there's that Aunt Daph stuff, plus she did mention the word "dead". So it's on my mind, because I can't hear anything in there, and for all I know she's lying there turning into stone, or dirt, or dust or whatever it is you turn into after you're dead, after the worms are done with you. If there's one thing I don't want, it's to be in a house with a dead person. I mean, "old" is bad enough.

I'm wondering if I should phone somebody, but I decide it's too soon. I mean, really, she's just been in there overnight. Maybe she's just sleeping in. But I go to the phone anyway and I'm going to call Maureen just to let her know where I am and the number, when I notice the leaf. It's Aunt Daph's leaf, the one that's made of porcelain and has red and silverflecks running through it. "You're going to break something," I can hear her, reading my tea leaves. She was right. My leg. What else did she say, about Aunt Flo? Oh yeah, pain. What she had to look forward to.

I go to the door and try begging for awhile.

"Aunt Florence? Please come out. Are you all right? . . . Would you make a noise or something so I know? Please?"

Nothing.

"Hey, like I'm really sorry if I upset you or anything, but I just want to know if you're okay. Should I call a doctor or something?"

There is a large thump in her room. I translate it to mean "no". This is encouraging. She's alive. She's responding.

"Well, is there anything you'd like me to do?"

No answer, just a great yawning silence.

Maybe she isn't alive. Maybe she just fell dead.

"Aunt Florence? Would you make another thumping noise or something? Aunt Florence?"

"Vater se plants ant feed se cat."

Her voice! Her voice! She actually spoke. "Yeah! Sure. No problem! I'll do that!"

"Ant talk to Jennifer."

"Yeah! I will!" It dawns on me. I thought we were alone. We *are* alone. "Who is Jennifer?"

"She's hanging above se sink," says the voice from the bedroom.

I've been reduced to talking to a plant. A plant hanging above the sink, its leafy tentacles groping the air for my voice. This is weird. This is something I do not do under normal circumstances. But then, these are not normal circumstances. I am doing it to get Aunt Florence out of her room. There is no other reason to talk to a plant, at least no other reason that I know of.

But first I water the jungle and feed the cat. Of course I have to do all this on crutches. I have to make up a new word for the way I get around.

I mean, you can't call it walking, it's crutching. I crutch my way around.

It takes me about three tea kettles of water to do all the plants, and a can of cat food to feed Willy the cat. You'd think he'd never been fed before, the way he goes after it — which is a laugh because he's the size of a small horse. You don't get to be that big if you're a starved cat. You don't get that big if you're a starved horse either. Anyway, I save talking to Jennifer for last. This is because I am trying to think of something to say. I mean, what do you say to a plant?

I look at Jennifer for a minute hanging there above the sink with three taps and decide she's actually pretty, which proves I'm going nuts because a plant is a plant. I mean, throw in a few leaves, stick it in a pot and what have you got? A plant. I pour some water into the pot, *her* pot (she is a she), and say, "Drink up," which, as far as I can tell, she does, because the water disappears.

Plants can be very quiet when they put their minds to it, which is exactly what Jennifer is doing. She doesn't make a sound. "How's it going?" I ask. No response. Maybe she's shy. "Are you shy?" I wait for an answer. Not even the quivering of a leaf. "You're very pretty for a plant," I try flattery, "but you're shy eh?" Still no answer. For some reason I get irritated. She's just stubborn, or stuck-up, like some people

I know. "All right, don't talk to me, see if I care." I crutch away.

I've just made an ass of myself. Talking to a plant. And expecting an answer.

I go over my life to this point in time, to now, and wonder just what it is that I've done wrong. It makes me wonder if there is a God. My parents never go to church, so I don't have much interest in it either, but I sure wonder sometimes. If there is a God, what does He do? Does He watch us on a big-screen TV, like we watch ants, wondering what we're going to do next? Does He switch channels? What does He do when He's bored? Watch us wreck the ozone layer? Golf? Does He have spare time? Is there time? Is He a She? Who knows? There's all kinds of people who say they know but I don't. How do they know? You feel so powerless sometimes, like there really is Somebody or Something in charge, and They're just playing around, doing things to you to see how you'll react. Maybe it's because of the way I always play with my milk that God has done this. This is His way of getting back at me. Maybe it's the way I hate those open and honest sessions that I have with my parents. Maybe it's what I did to Boog. I don't know. I feel guilty, like everything is my fault.

"I'm done," I tell the door, hoping that whoever's on the other side will come out, or at least answer me. "Aunt Florence? I'm done," I repeat.

"Vat did she say?"

"Who?" This surprises me. I wasn't talking to anyone.

"Jennifer."

Oh, the plant "The plant?!"

"Yes, vat did she say?" says the voice behind the door.

"I don't know, nothing! Plants don't talk!" I mean, give me a break.

"Yes, sey do."

"Aunt Florence, plants don't talk. I mean, they don't talk."

"Yes, sey do."

"No, they don't." I'm arguing with a door.

"Vell, sey talk to me."

Is everybody crazy? "They don't have tongues!"

And here she yells something at me in German. I have no idea what she's saying, so I yell back the only German word I know. It's a word my Dad calls his brother Mike.

"*Schaskopf!*" I yell. It's the only German word I know. "*Schafskopf*" literally means "sheephead", which not-so-literally means "idiot". I've blown it. I should have said, "Yeah, we talked about the weather, the state of the universe, and the price of tea in China." But I didn't. I called her a sheephead instead.

Not the thing to say. Especially to an German aunt who has locked herself in her bedroom. I try pleading for a while.

"Aunt Florence, I'm sorry. Please come out. Ple-ease?"

Nothing.

"Aunt Florence, is there anything I can do to make you come out? I mean, anything at all. I'm sorry I'm such a jerk."

Nothing. I try worrying her.

"What happens if the house burns down? Then what?"

I hear some rustling noises from in her room. That did it. I've got her out, she's coming.

But instead, a piece of paper slides under the door. On it is printed one word. "*TOUGH*," it says.

Great. Just great. Now what? I should phone someone. Yeah, but who? And what should I say? "Ah, my aunt's locked herself in her bedroom because I said her plants don't talk." Right. "My aunt's locked in her bedroom because some old fart wouldn't take her to a concert." Su-ure. Who's going to understand that? Aunt Daph? Save me. She's having enough trouble saving herself. Shawna — she's got to be back. My finger sticks in the dial.

"'Lo?" a man's voice answers.

"Hello, Shawna there?"

"Wrong number, bud." The phone clicks.

I redial. The phone rings, once, twice... five times. No answer. Shit. She's not back yet.

Maureen. Maureen will understand. If she doesn't, I'll just be more depressed, if you can be more depressed on top of being depressed.

I dial her number, carefully.

"Hello?" says the other end of the line. Her father.

"Hi, can I speak to Maureen please?"

"Who is this?"

"It's Lanny... Reich."

"I'm sorry Lanny, but Maureen can't come to the phone right now. I'm afraid she's been grounded for a couple of weeks."

"Two weeks? Oh. I see. Well, Merry Christmas," I say.

"Same to you," he says.

Grounded, for two weeks. What did she do to deserve that? Probably something to do with Boog, she probably went out with him or something and got caught. And I think I got troubles. I *do* got troubles! Have troubles. Who can I call? Forget Uncle Mike, he's a write-off. Aunt Daph's in no position for this kind of call, and the same applies to Grandma and Grandpa. I can't phone anyone. I am now depressed on top of being depressed.

I decide to do the only thing I can do.

I'll outwait her.

I'll outwait the Grand Old Dame.

* * *

The trouble with waiting is that it takes so long. I hate it. There's nothing to do. I crutch over to one of the bookshelves and stare. All those books. And I've read all the English ones. Both of them, not including Dad's. I take them down.

This is no easy going, I tell you. Reading poetry is like reading another language, only worse. You recognize the words, but you can't make any sense of how they're put together. It reminds me of Shakespeare in school. I know we're supposed to read the actual play, but I just get the *Coles Notes* and pretend I've read it. It's quicker and you can usually fake your way through on a test. Everybody does it, except for the weirdos, who read everything. On the other hand, this year we read a play called *King Lear*. And the stupid book store was sold out of *Coles Notes* for it. So I rented the video and we read parts of it in class. And I couldn't help thinking of this guy I know, Jack Leier, who plays on our team, and wonder if it's an ancient relative of his. I hope not, because this King Lear is really heavy duty. He has this scene on a heath, which I think is like an open space of prairie, where he goes nutso in a major way. He gets so upset over how things are with his three daughters that he gouges out his eyes. I get kind of confused by all the characters and stuff, but in the end I feel like someone pulled the plug and I've been drained.

Why I'm thinking about all this, I don't know, but I'm sort of leafing through one of Dad's books when I come to this one poem that catches my eye: "Doggerel for Lanny My Son", it says. I didn't know he wrote a poem for me. How come he never told me about it? This is it.

> First you danced in your mother's womb,
> Then squealing you danced on my knee.
> I remember you dancing with Mr. Raisin,
> His violin and cats in glee.
> You danced to any sound you heard
> And sometimes to silence, in a net.
> Now you dance when you score a goal
> A ritual on ice that you've set.
> I fear you will dance only a dance or two more
> Then become leaden like me
> And dance only when you've been waiting too long
> And can't find a place to pee.

At least he didn't steal, except for Mr. Raisin's name, which I gave him. Dad probably thinks this poem is kind of funny, and maybe it is, except that the kind of mood I'm in, nothing's funny. It really sounds like he's sad about something, "become leaden like me." In fact, if you take away the last line, it is sad. He's sad about me growing up, or me being like him. Don't worry, Dad, I won't be a thief.

I put Dad's books back on the shelf and pull down another. Willy the cat rubs up against me as I'm looking at it. It's old and dusty with German writing on the inside page and music notes on hand drawn lines. Somebody had a lot of patience to do all this. The cat doesn't stick around long and jumps up on the piano and starts licking his back leg. You get the feeling he's showing off how flexible he is, when it occurs to me that in my very hands might be the key to opening Aunt Flo's door. I don't mean it as a pun because I can't figure out which key this thing is written in, but if I try to play it, maybe she'll think I'm interested in music and come out to help me.

I go to the piano and set this book down. The cat looks at me.

I start to play. The cat leaves.

I bang away for about half an hour and I've got the first two bars sort of figured out, but it's not going well and it sounds awful. I mean, really bad. If anyone needs help, I do. So I go to Aunt Flo's door, getting ready to do a begging routine, when I see there's already a message on the floor waiting for me. It says,

WRONG KEY

"Well, what key's it supposed to be in?" I ask the door.

The door does not respond.

YULETIDE BLUES

"Aw, come on, Aunt Florence. Give me a hand. Help me."

There's some scribbling noise from behind the door. A note appears:

WRITE SONATA

"Write a sonata? I can't even *play* one! How am I going to write one?" I don't really expect an answer here, and of course, I don't get one. But I think I've made progress. I mean, here's a specific task, and if I do it she'll come out, right?

I don't know if you've ever written music before, but let me tell you something, it's no piece of cake. First of all, you have to have notes that you can hear in your mind, and then you got to know how to write them down, which I don't, because I don't *want* to know. I couldn't care less. But I am not doing this for myself, right? I am doing this to get my aunt out of the bedroom. So I *try*. That's all I can do is *try*. If I could *do* it, that'd be that, presto, done. *Trying* is one of those great things you can spend your whole life doing and never getting anything done. It's like taking those steps, you know, if you take one step, then take half of that step, and half of that step, and half of that step, and so on, you eventually never get anywhere. You just keep halfing things to infinity. So anyway, trying to write a sonata is sort of like that, taking steps to infinity. I've come up with an idea. I am half-way to infinity. End of day five.

It takes me most of the night, but I do it. I write what I think is a sonata. It's not very long. In fact it's very short. What do you expect for a first try? I made it. It's mine. The only thing I stole was the first four notes from "Silent Night." I mean, she should be able to relate to that, right? I sign it, go to the door, slide it under, and wait.

You won't believe what happens. I mean, I go through all the trouble of figuring out what a sonata is and then I write one because she, the Grand Old Dame, says so. Then what does she do? She sends me a note:

NOT GOOD ENOUGH

I croak, "What do you mean, not good enough?!! Who do you think I am? Beethoven? You want a sonata, write your own and stop feeling so sorry for yourself. I mean, think of me! I got a broken leg and I'm stuck here with you!!"

As soon as I say that, I know it is not the thing to say. I could live to regret this. The cat strolls by, glares at me, on his way to his food dish. All the vegetables stare me down. As usual they're not saying much, but I'm getting the message anyway. "Creep," they're saying.

I am a creep. I am suddenly very cold and my leg hurts. All my life things have been so easy

214 YULETIDE BLUES

for me. Nothing's ever really gone wrong, I mean for me, personally. My parents have always been so protective, looking after me, sheltering me, limiting me to all these half-steps. I've never had a crisis. The question is this: how am I going to know I can handle trouble when it comes? I've never been tested. I think this is it. This is my chance to prove I can handle anything and get G.O.D. out of her room.

I'll burn down the house.

Chapter twenty-two

I am excited about this idea of burning down the house. The only problem is that it's crazy. It's crazy that I should even think about it. I should really call someone. Shawna. She's got to be back by now.

I dial her number. While I dial, I'm afraid that she will simply hang up like she has done a dozen times before. What the heck am I going to say?

"Hello?" Her voice, her incredibly beautiful voice.

"Please don't hang up," I blurt. There is a pause. She hasn't hung up. "I'm at my aunt's. She's in her room. I broke my leg. I'm going to burn down the house. I'm sorry for what I said to you. Please forgive me. I like you a lot." I say all this pretty fast. She still hasn't hung up.

"You're going to burn down the house?"

"To get her out of her room. She won't come out. I've tried everything. She won't come out."

"You can't burn down the house, Lanny. That's stupid."

"I know. I'm going nuts."

"Yeah," she says.

"How are you?" I ask. I don't know why I ask, but I do.

"I'm fine. How are *you*?"

"I'm fine," I lie. I try to balance the lie with a truth. "It's really good to hear your voice," I say, "it really is."

"Lanny, don't burn down the house. I mean, what's going on?"

"Aunt Daph, you know my Aunt Daphne? She tried to commit suicide, so I'm here with my other aunt, Aunt Florence, and she got all depressed and she locked herself in her room."

"Suicide?"

"Yeah."

"Oh, Lanny."

"I know, I know." What do I know?

"Can't you call someone?"

"I am, I did, I'm calling you."

"But like, I mean, someone in your family."

"No. Who?"

"Your grandparents?"

"They wouldn't understand and I mean, what could they do?"

"Well, they could do *something*. I mean, besides burning down the house."

"Yeah, but what?"

"I don't know!" She's a bit cheesed off.

"I want to do this myself. I have to do this myself."

"Why?"

"I just have to, that's all."

"What do you have to do yourself?"

"I have to work it out by myself?"

"Why?"

This is going nowhere. This is going in circles. "I don't know. I just do."

"Well then, why are you asking me for help?"

"I'm not asking you for help."

"Yes, you are."

"No, I'm not."

"Then what are you doing?"

"I don't know. I just wanted to tell you."

There is a long pause. Willy the cat strolls in. He looks up at me. I've never noticed it before, but he's sort of shaped like a violin. He jumps on my lap. "Ow!" I say.

"What's the matter?"

"Cat just jumped on my lap. Had his claws out."

"Good. I hope he dug in deep."

"Gee, thanks!"

"Do you know why I didn't talk to you? Why I kept hanging up on you?"

"Yeah." I quickly reconsider. "No, why?"

"Because you always get your way. If I had talked to you, you would say you're sorry, and that would be it. I would forgive you, and you would have your way. And everything would be hunky-dory."

"Yeah?" I fail to see what's wrong with this.

"Well, it's not okay. You can't go calling people whatever you like and expect everything to be fine just because you say you're sorry."

"But I am sorry." I am.

"You don't understand, do you?"

"No."

This goes on for awhile, me not understanding what's so wrong with being sorry and her explaining. Finally we start to get somewhere.

"Well, then what exactly do you mean when you say you're sorry?"

"I mean it's my fault, you're innocent, it was wrong for me to call you that and we're both equal and it's okay to make mistakes," I say, covering all the arguments.

"Then why did you call me a slut?" It may take her a minute or two, but she always comes to the point.

"I don't know, because I really like you. And if I really like *you*, Shawna, the person, then how can I hurt you? So I call you a slut, and you're not Shawna anymore, just a thing, then I can hurt you. If you want to hurt someone, you turn them into a thing first. So that's what I did to you. I turned you into a thing, a slut." As I say this, this is a whole realization for me. I knew I was sorry, but I didn't know why. I was sorry for treating her like a thing, not like a person. And I do it all the time, not just to her, but to everybody. And everybody does it to everybody else. It goes on and on till you even get wars. You kill gooks and krauts, *things*, not people. It's hard to hurt people. "That's what I'm sorry for, I'm sorry for turning you into a thing. Nobody wants to be a thing. Nobody is a thing."

"Thank you, Lanny. I think that's the first time anybody ever really apologized to me."

"I'm not apologizing, it just occurred to me. I mean, thank *you*."

"Guess what?"

"What?"

"I have to go now. My dad wants to use the phone."

"Okay. Well, call me later. Or I'll call you."

"Don't burn down the house," she says and hangs up.

Okay, I feel better now. Better than I've felt in days, weeks, maybe even months. But I still have the problem of getting Aunt Florence out of her room. I won't burn down the house. I'll just start a little fire.

I collect some of the paper I wrote on and put it in one of her stainless steel bowls from the kitchen. Just for flavour, I add a few plant leaves. Hopefully they'll make a lot of smoke. I set it in front of her door and look for matches. I can't find any. I look everywhere. I practically turn the place upside-down — no matches. Then I remember a trick Mom uses when she want to light one of her cancer sticks but can't find a light. I go to the toaster, turn it on and wait till the elements glow. I torch some paper. We now have fire.

This is it, the big test, not that I'm actually going to burn the house to the ground, just give the impression I am, to scare her out of her room.

I light the paper and the leaves in the bowl, and sure enough, it starts smoking like a forest fire. This is going to be good, but just as I try to fan the smoke under the G.O.D.'s door, Willy the cat shows up. He wants to see what's going on and if you want to know how curiosity killed the cat, this is a fairly good example. Picture this: I'm fanning the smoke, yelling, "Fire! Fire!" and this cat is strolling by checking things out, when suddenly G.O.D.'s door flies open and there she sits in her wheelchair with a large red tank on her lap. It's a fire extinguisher and before I can make a peep, there is a huge explosion of white gunk that shoots out of the nozzle onto the bowl of paper and leaves. And Willy the cat. You have never seen any living thing move so fast. Dead things, yeah, like lightning or bullets, but never something living, like a cat. He moves so fast, in fact, that Aunt Florence doesn't even see him.

She slams the door shut and all again is quiet, except for the sound of my heart beating.

I hobble over to the fridge to find Willy in his hiding place. I know that's where he's going to be and sure enough, two eyes glow at me from the dark corner behind the fridge. "Here kitty," I say, "come on Willy, kitty kitty." Of course he doesn't move. He stays there like a bump on a log. Then a scary thing happens. Willy's eyes go out. I mean, like they stop glowing. He's closed them, or turned them off or something. I call a couple more times but you might as well talk to the wall. I get the broom and try poking him out. I can sort of feel him, soft, but no reaction. I go to the closet and find an umbrella. I try hooking the handle around the cat. I get him. I pull him out.

Willy is dead.

Chapter twenty-three

Now I know this might gross you out, but I feel very strange about this. I mean, I'm not used to handling death. A little while ago, this was just a kitty-cat, leaving hair all over the place. Now it's dead. And I do something I don't know I can do. I give Willy the dead cat mouth-to-mouth resuscitation. I put his nose and mouth in my mouth and give little huffs of breath at about the rate I think cats normally breathe. And while I'm doing this I'm not thinking about anything, my mind is totally calm and blank. I just do it. I'm huffing into the body of a dead cat. If you thought about it, you wouldn't do it.

The cat starts breathing by itself. I get a towel and try to wipe it off because it's kind of wet and stuff. I think about getting a blow-dryer but the poor cat is obviously freaked enough. I wonder how old he is. Willy has been around as long as I can remember. I should stop thinking because I somehow rub the cat the wrong way and he digs his claws into my hand and uses it as a launching pad to take off away from me. That's gratitude. Way to say thanks, Willy. G.O.D doesn't know either, I mean that I saved her cat's life. What'd have happened if the stupid thing died? How could I have explained that one? Actually, probably easier than explaining how I brought it back to life.

I'm in the process of trying to clean things up a bit, wondering what to do, when the phone rings. The house is very quiet right abouts now, so the ringing sounds incredibly loud and scares me half to death. It's a real "ring", not one of those electronic tonal-sounding "wawa's". My leg hurts. I hobble to the phone. "Hello?"

"Lanny?" says a voice from another planet.

"Hi Dad, how are you?" He has impeccable timing.

"I'm fine, we're fine. How are things with you and Aunt Flo?"

"Oh, they're okay I guess. I mean I went and broke my leg in a hockey game."

"You what?! He broke his leg. How?"

"I told you. In a game. I fell into the boards."

"He fell into the boards." This is getting relayed to Mom, but it won't be good enough for her. "Here's Mom."

"What happened?" asks Mom.

"I broke my leg. I fell into the boards," I repeat.

"Are you okay?"

"No, I'm not okay. I've got a broken leg."

"But aside from that."

"Yeah, well. Yeah, I'm okay." Lying has never been my strong suit.

"You don't sound okay."

"Well, ah . . . " Should I tell her?

"What?"

"Aunt Florence locked herself in her room," I tell her.

"She what?!"

"She locked . . . "

"I heard what you said, I want to know why? What's going on?"

"I don't know."

"You don't know?!" She screeches this loud enough to knock a couple antennas off whatever satellite is bouncing this phone signal across the planet. I think she knows it too, because she repeats it again, quieter, and somehow more menacing. "You don't know?" She's PO'd.

"Well, I *know*, but it's a long story."

"Tell it."

"The whole thing?"

"Everything." She's really PO'd.

"Well, I guess it all started with the cat, you know, Willy?"

"Yes, I know Willy — what's wrong with Willy?"

"Well, nothing, now. I mean he's alive — I brought him back to life."

"What happened?"

"He was covered in foam. He must have had a heart attack."

"What do you mean? What are you talking about, foam? Who had a heart attack?"

"The cat, Willy, from a fire extinguisher, we had a fire." About now it dawns on me that this isn't really good news to tell your mother when she can't do anything about anything. "But hey," I continue, trying to impress her, "everything's going to be all right. I wrote a sonata."

"Let me talk to Florence!" She fails to be impressed.

"Well, I'll call her, but I doubt if she'll come."

"Lan, get her on the phone."

"I think she's having a nap."

"Right now!" From two thousand miles away I can tell she means business.

I call. "Aunt Florence? Aunt Florence, will you come to the phone? It's my Mom and Dad." I wait. "They're calling long-distance. They want to talk to you." Nothing. "She's not coming," I say to the phone.

"She's not coming? Why Lanny?! Is she sick?" Now she's not PO'd anymore. It's *panic time*. "Is she *alive*?"

"Oh yeah, of course she's alive, she's fine. She's just depressed because some old guy wouldn't take her to a concert."

There's silence on the other end of the phone. The kind of silence that makes you wonder if you're deaf. "Mom?"

"Do you want us to come home?"

She wants to take care of her baby boy. "No, Mom, it's okay. There's nothing to worry about. Things always sound worse than they are."

"You call your Uncle Mike. No, never mind, I'll call him."

"No, Mom, don't please. Really, I can handle it. I *want* to handle it. You'll be back in a week and everything'll be fine."

"If she won't come out of her room, something is very wrong and I'm not going to leave it up to you to *handle* it."

"Don't you trust me?"

"No."

They never trust me. They never believe me. "Fine. Do what you like."

"Don't take that attitude with me."

"I just said fine."

"I know what you said. I'm calling Mike and . . ."

"Just a second." I interrupt her, because suddenly the bedroom door swings open and guess who rolls out. "Here's . . . " Aunt Florence takes the phone from my hand.

"Hello? Colleen?" she says. "How are you?" She pauses, listening to Mom. Mom is no doubt trying to ask what's going on without sounding upset. She's a social worker. She should be good at it. "No, everysing is fine," says G.O.D.

I can't believe this!

They babble on some more about the weather and stuff, and she hangs up without even giving me a chance to say good-bye.

She turns to go.

"Thanks," I say, not meaning it.

"You're velcome," she says, not meaning it.

"Why'd you say everything's all right?" I'm a little bugged here.

"Vat?" she says, like she's surprised.

"Why did you say everything was all right, was 'fine', when you've been locking yourself in your room handing me notes under the door and maybe starving yourself to death for all I know?"

"Excuse me," she says and tries to go by me in her wheelchair. I poke my cast in the way. Where does she think she's going? I want to have this out, now.

"Excuse me," she says again.

"No," I say. "I want an answer. Why'd you say everything was all right?"

"I didn't vant her to vorry," she says, clipping every word like scissors.

"You didn't want her to worry! Why not?!"

"Because she's two sousand miles avay."

"So?" I like to be concise.

"So sere's nosing she can do about it."

I hate it when people are logical and reasonable, because they usually miss the point.

"There's nothing I can do about it either," I say, "and I'm right here."

She struggles a bit to get by. My cast makes a good road block.

"I vant to go to my room," she says. I know this is going to sound ridiculous right now, but she reminds me of me. I decide to play Dad.

"Okay, go." I move. "But don't expect me to co-operate." I have no idea what this means. I just say it because it's the only thing that comes to mind. It slows her for a second though. I mean she stops for a sec and eyeballs me.

"You tried to burn down se house."

"I put some paper in front of your door. It was in a bowl. It wasn't going to hurt nothing. I wanted to get you out of your room."

"Vell, it didn't vork did it."

"No, it didn't." She starts rolling to her room. "It just about killed the cat."

She stops. "Vat do you mean?"

"With that squirter of yours, the fire extinguisher, you got Willy."

"Vere is he?"

"I don't know. Check behind the fridge."

She does an about face in her chair and almost does a wheely heading to the kitchen. "Villy! Villy!" she calls. The cat, of course, does not respond. He may have had a relapse. I gimp to the kitchen. G.O.D. is poking around with the umbrella. "Here kitty, come on Villy," she's saying.

"Are his eyes lit?" I ask.

"Vat?"

"Can you see his eyes?"

"No."

"Oh no. Here, let me." I haul the cat out. Dead. How can the same cat die twice in the same hour? I do mouth-to-mouth again. "Vat are you doing? Vat are you doing?" I hear Aunt Flo say. I don't stop to tell her. I keep doing it.

After about five minutes I stop. "It worked the first time," I say.

"You did sis before?"

"Yeah," I say, "I'm sorry. It's my fault. You squirted him but it wouldn't have happened if I hadn't lit the fire."

She doesn't say anything. She just strokes the dead wet cat on her lap. I decide I should leave the two of them alone for awhile, but as I start to crutch off, she says, "Sere's a box, a cardboard box in the back porch. Get it." I know immediately that this is meant to be the coffin, and I wonder how and where I'm going to dig a hole, a grave, to put him in. You'd need a pick and blow torch to get through the frozen ground. As if she reads my mind, Aunt Florence says, "Ve'll call se SPCA. Sey'll take him avay."

* * *

230 YULETIDE BLUES

I don't care if it's day or night anymore and to tell the truth, I hardly notice. The guys from the SPCA came and got Willy. Nobody said much. Aunt Flo signed something and said it was his time; he was seventeen. I lie here on the bed wondering when *my* time is. And when Aunt Flo's is. She's a lot more than seventeen.

I hear a funny sound coming from Aunt Flo's bedroom and slowly going to the kitchen. It's a regular thumping noise followed by some shuffling. I can't figure out what it is. It's weird enough to make me get up and have a look.

There in the kitchen is Aunt Flo. She's standing with the umbrella in her hand. No wheelchair.

"What are you doing?" I ask.

"Making tea," she says, plugging in the electric kettle.

"Where's your wheelchair?" I ask.

"I don't need it to make tea," she says and thumps the umbrella on the floor using it as a cane, shuffling in little tiny steps after it. Each time she thumps the umbrella it's like the world is going to stop before she takes her little shuffle steps, as though she's trying to tell herself it doesn't hurt. She is very teetery. She crosses the kitchen this way to the cupboard. There she reaches up and grabs a box of tea. All I can do is watch. "Do you vant some?" she asks.

"No. Yeah," I say, not sure if I do want tea but remembering that I should "try and be nice".

"I'm going to valk from now on," she says. "I'm going to valk until I fall into my grave."

We're sitting there at the kitchen table waiting for the tea to steep. This is the most fun I've had in a week, except it hasn't been a week, only six days. The whole notion of fun, the whole idea or concept, just doesn't exist for me any more. When we've sat there for about an hour, Aunt Flo takes the cover off the pot and starts to pour.

"Do you take milk?" she asks.

"Yeah," I say, "sugar too." Anything to hide the taste of tea.

"You know vere it is," she says.

I get up and hobble to the fridge and as I open the door, I think of Willy who helped me clean up the mess I made two days ago. I think of all the milk I spilled in my life. I think of the doodling I've done with it. I think of Mom and Dad. I take the milk and hobble back to the table. I set the carton beside my cup. "I can handle it," I think to myself, not that I can think to anyone else. I open the carton and pour. Milk is beautiful to watch while it pours. They squeeze it out of cows and put it in cartons so you can watch it pour.

"Oops."

I've slopped it over the edge of the cup. It doesn't matter because there's a saucer underneath. Technically this is not spilt milk.

"Sis is not vorking out," says Aunt Florence.

"What?" I don't know what she's talking about.

"Your staying here is not vorking out."

This stuns me. I mean, I know it's true, but now I'm going to get booted out into the snow. How much worse can things get? It's only another few days. I don't know what to say. And for a change, I don't say anything.

"It's only a few days," she says, reading my mind. "You can go stay mit your Uncle Mike."

I take a sip of tea. It's all I can do.

CHAPTER TWENTY-FOUR

My bags, such as they are, are packed. I've taken off my hockey pants, had a bath and sacrificed a pair of jeans to the cause of my cast by cutting the outside seam almost to my waist so I can fit my leg into it. We're waiting for Uncle Mike. Dad is not going to be pleased. I don't blame him.

I'm actually sitting on the piano stool. It's a short hobble from here to the door and when I have to leave, it'll be the path of least resistance. Out of sheer and utter boredom I turn around and lift the piano lid. I tinkle with the keys. I try to play those bars I wrote for G.O.D. It just doesn't happen. I can't do it. The problem, I realize, is that it's not my kind of music. I wrote it to try and please Aunt Flo. But I like the notes, I mean, the notes themselves actually sound okay. They would make a good melody, if you like Christmas carols.

I play around with them. I give them a different tempo, a different rhythm. It's amazing what the same notes sound like if you give different spaces between them. And all those keys are in front of me. I've never noticed there's so many before, and depending how you

BLUES

...ou can make a whole lot of music. ...usic I'm making sounds sort of like ...ewood, like blues. You can recognize the ...elody, but it's different, I'm making it up as I go.

But that's not what I'm thinking, or only part of what I'm thinking, because what's really on my mind is what an incredibly stupid couple of weeks this has been, about Boog, Shawna, everybody. Especially Aunt Daph. And I'm playing the piano thinking of this stuff. All of a sudden, I'm aware of the fact that I'm playing the piano and I get that feeling you get when you ride a bike for the first time. You're up there, rolling and you just want to go forever. And it actually seems like forever till you see a fence coming, or a curb. So you try to turn, and you do, and turning is even more exciting than getting rolling in the first place because you're rolling *and* turning. For the first time in my life, I am really playing the piano. And now I understand why they call it "playing" because that's what it is. Playing the blues.

But just like riding the bike, there's fences in piano playing too. Through the blues, I hear Aunt Flo, I hear the fence, "thump shuffle-shuffle, thump shuffle-shuffle." I turn my music and keep on rolling. I look up and she's standing there. She's smiling. She nods. I'm finally doing something right.

"That's not good enough, you got to promise you're going to give them to me, piano lessons, technique and stuff."

"If I liff, und if you liff."

* * *

My parents arrived home. Dad actually got a tan. On his forehead and bald spot. Mom said she never got up the nerve to wear her new bathing suit. It was good to see them. But they were not too thrilled about all that happened. I kind of make up for it by volunteering to do the visiting in the hospital. We've made a home of it, me in a cast pushing this old gal around in a wheelchair, following Aunt Daph to the canteen or wherever. Sometimes Shawna joins us. Aunt Florence is still cranky from time to time, but who wouldn't be, shackled to a wheelchair. In a couple of weeks she can go home again, to her piano.

One of Shawna's cats had kittens. It wasn't supposed to but it did. We've already got one picked out. I'm going to bring it over to Aunt Flo's the next time I go for lessons.